Alberto Moravia was born in Rome in 1907, the son of an architect. He wrote his first novel in 1925, and then became foreign correspondent in London, Paris and elsewhere for *La Stampa* and *Gazzetta del Popolo* of Turin. In the later years of Fascism his books were banned and he had to write articles under a pseudonym. During the German occupation of Italy he went into hiding in the mountains, being liberated by the Americans in May 1944. He lives in Rome and Capri and is incontestably Italy's best-known and most popular writer of fiction.

THE VOYEUR

REVIEWS

'Moving' – *The Observer*

'Gripping' – *City Limits*

'Lucidity that dazzles' – *The Guardian*

'A quality read' – *Literary Review*

'Moravia handles his material with consummate skill, weaving a complex web of feeling and reaction . . . sensitive and sympathetic' – *Forum Magazine*

Also by Alberto Moravia and published by
Futura:

EROTIC TALES

ALBERTO MORAVIA

THE VOYEUR

Translated from the Italian by Tim Parks

Futura

Contents

CHAPTER ONE

An Ordinary Day in my Life, as Prologue

∽✦∾

Six-thirty a.m. I don't sleep long, not more than six hours a night, and as soon as I'm awake I devote five or ten minutes to that rare occupation that goes under the name of thinking. What do I think about? Coming out with it cold like this, it could well seem ridiculous: about the end of the world. I don't know when or how this habit began: not so long ago perhaps, after reading a book I came across on my father's desk – he's a physics professor at the university – one of those endless books about nuclear war. Or maybe there was another reason, one that came from I don't know where and then disappeared from my memory, the way a seed disappears when the plant has grown. But then it's not quite correct to say that I think about nuclear war. If anything I think of the impossibility of thinking about it. Still, what is certain is that in those five or ten minutes after waking up, I don't think of anything else.

I should also say that those few minutes in the early

morning when I think about the bomb are maybe the only time in the day when I do get round to doing any real, that is abstract, thinking. This is because I live most of all through my eyes and those ten minutes are the only ones in twenty-four hours when I find myself in a situation conducive to thought: in the dark, doing nothing and, crucially, with nothing to look at. The rest of the day I'm always doing something or looking at something, and doing and looking prevent me from thinking. But then aren't five or ten minutes thinking enough for one day? It didn't take long, for example, for this thinking about the end of the world to become obsessive. During the day I do forget about it, it's true; but the moment I wake up, twenty-four hours later, I find to my amazement that the thought is still there, immutable, threatening, and above all unthinkable.

Seven o'clock. I get up, taking care not to wake Silvia who's asleep beside me. Completely naked and barefoot (I've never had pyjamas, dressing gown or slippers, I don't know why, perhaps it's an unconscious rebellion against bourgeois hedonism), I walk through to the poky, irregular-shaped little bathroom my father had fitted out for my wife and myself in a corner of his huge flat. There's no bath, just a shower at the point where the slanting ceiling is at its lowest: Silvia's smaller than me and can stand under the water with her head up, but I'm taller and have to bend down.

After showering, I wipe the steam off the room's small window with a gesture that's become a habit and look out across the courtyard and up above the straight, bare walls at the sky to see what the weather's doing. Then I stand in front of the mirror over the sink.

Which brings me to the question of shaving: should I, or shouldn't I? I have a thick, tough beard and it's hard to shave; added to which I'm lazy and tend to let things go, so that I more or less end up shaving alternate days. While weighing up the pros and cons of whether to shave or not, I take the opportunity to look at myself in the mirror: my reflection intrigues me, as though it belonged to somebody else.

I'm a good-looking man of thirty-five, but I'm not a handsome man: it's an important distinction. My features are at once virile and weak: my eyes are light blue with a searching, often ironic gaze, but with eyebrows that lack energy and have a downward turn to them; my nose is straight and decisive, but it wrinkles about the nostrils in a finicky expression; my mouth has white, sharp, wolfish teeth, but the lips are fleshy and soft; my hair is black and has life to it, but is already getting thin over the forehead and round the temples; my chin begins with a show of will perhaps, but then folds over on itself to form a little dimple in the middle. What else? I'd like to take a look at the rest of my body, but the mirror is too high; until I move house I'll be restricted to seeing nothing but my face of a morning.

Still, I do see the rest of my body soon after dressing when I walk through the hall and glance in passing at the dark, scratched mirror that looms over the console. With a mixture of irritation and self-satisfaction I recognize myself there as that particular kind of person usually described as an "intellectual". Yes, I'm an intellectual. If from nothing else you can tell straight off from the way I dress, just as in the Middle Ages it seems you could tell an altar boy from the clothes he wore. I have a dark blue shirt, black tie, a brown or blue pullover, green or brown cord jacket with leather elbow patches, jeans or grey flannel trousers, and those dark suede, so-called "desert" shoes. But what really gives me away as an intellectual is the shabby, tired look these clothes have: the leather elbow patches are shiny, the shirt is worn out, the tie old and twisted, the trousers lost their creases way back. Anyway, apart from this outfit, all I have is one blue suit for special occasions: ceremonies, official reunions, receptions, etc.

Seven-thirty a.m. As soon as I'm dressed, I go down to the narrow street in this old part of Rome where our block is located and walk to the kiosk at the corner to get my father's papers. Since the serious car accident which has kept him bed-ridden for three months now, I do this and various other little chores for him, things I'd never have dreamt of doing "before". Why do I write "before" in inverted commas? Because since the day of the accident I have been discovering that as well as being an intellectual, I am also a son.

But wasn't I a son "before", too? Yes and no. For the purposes of the official registry, I was. But in my heart I felt my father was a complete stranger and I liked it that way. So why the change? Quite honestly, because of a look, a single look that my father gave me on the stairs the day of the accident.

That morning the ramshackle lift in our block was, as usual, out of order. So I started down the dark solemn stairway with its shallow steps of polished travertine and huge landings ornamented with busts of classical heroes. Then, on the last flight, I saw an unusual group coming towards me: two men carrying a stretcher with a third man lying on it. I moved to one side, I hadn't seen it was my father yet. But as the stretcher came level with me, I heard someone call my name and realized it was him. On his back, wrapped in a blanket up to his chin, his magnificent white hair all tousled and his usually sanguine complexion now intensely pale, he shot me a quick look, as if to reassure himself I'd recognized him; then, with an

4

attempt at a smile, he said: "It's nothing, your run-of-the-mill car accident, I got off pretty lightly." The bearers, who had stopped when he called me, began to climb again and without a word I turned round and followed them up the stairs.

I suppose you'll want to know what kind of look it was that prompted this change in my relationship with my father. Well, it wasn't the look a father gives his son, no, it was the look a man in pain turns to another man. A curious contradiction: this look of one man to another had the effect that from then on, I began to behave towards him as a son to a father.

I go up to the flat and into the kitchen. It's an old post-war-style kitchen: two big cupboards with flaking white paint, a complicated, cumbersome cooker, a large table with a marble top, chairs with wickerwork seats, and, in the middle of all this antiquated furniture, an enormous, spanking-new fridge. The kitchen is shadowy because its only light comes from a single narrow window which opens into the courtyard. I switch on the light and set about preparing my father's breakfast.

True, I could make my father wait another half an hour; at eight o'clock Rita, the old nurse who sleeps in the room next to his, will be around. And then obviously I could have the woman – she usually comes at ten to clean and make lunch, leaving in the evening after getting dinner – I could have her come earlier. But it's worth noting, if we're to understand this new and strange relationship between myself and my father, that right from the beginning there was a tacit agreement between us that it would be me who got him his breakfast, as though to underline precisely this change that took place after the accident.

So, very carefully, I cut a few slices of bread and slip them into the toaster; I put the coffee-pot on the burner; I lay a tray with a cup, milk, butter, honey, a carton of yoghurt and, what else? Oh yes, the paper napkins, I'm always forgetting the napkins. While the bread toasts and the coffee boils, I sit at the table and glance through the papers. Then a smell of hot bread fills the kitchen and the coffee bubbles over; I jump off my chair, turn off the burner, put the toast on a plate, place the two papers sideways across the tray, pick everything up and go out. As I walk, slowly so as not to upset the tray, along the narrow, twisting book-lined corridor that links the kitchen end of the flat where my two rooms are, to the other end where my father lives: as, to put it bluntly, I play waiter, I tell myself once again that taking my father his breakfast is one of the things I'd never have dreamt of doing before the accident, and above all something I'd never have dreamt of doing without being bored, but, on the contrary, with a remarkable show of filial devotion, too scrupulous perhaps to be truly sincere.

I find my father already awake, sitting up in bed in his pyjamas, leaning back on two pillows and tidying his hair with a comb and mirror he always keeps close to hand. He'll have the nurse give him his proper wash and brush-up after breakfast, but until then he takes care not to let himself be seen with his hair in a mess.

My father has arranged for the nurse to sleep in the adjoining bedroom, which is fairly small, and to have his own bed moved into the much larger study between the two windows. It is to these windows that, having combed his hair, he now turns his attention to see what's going on, or rather, what isn't going on, above the roofs of Rome. "Good morning," I say, "how are you?" and without turning he answers, "Not so bad." Then after a moment he turns and makes a downward gesture with his hand: "If you would." I understand and set down the tray on the trolley, pushing the whole thing forward as far as his chest; then I bend down, reach under the bed and pick up the glass container with the vaguely bird-like shape, known in Italy as a "parrot". By now it will be full of urine; sometimes it's still warm. I take hold of it about half-way down and, carrying it slightly away from me, go to empty it down the toilet. Every time I perform this task, which no one has asked me to do, but which I wouldn't let anyone else do, I find myself watching my reflection in the bathroom mirror and notice that I have a – how can I describe it? – remorseful look on my face. So I wonder whether, albeit unconsciously, I mightn't have a desire to punish myself, to atone. But to punish myself for what, atone for what?

I come back from the bathroom with the bottle carefully rinsed and put it under the bed within reach of my father. Then I sit down on an armchair opposite him. I don't eat breakfast with my father. I have the somewhat absurd habit of breakfasting later on in the bar in the street below our block. So while my father eats there's nothing for me to do but watch him. I watch him with particular attention, almost as if, by observing his face, I hoped to discover the real reason behind my changed attitude towards him.

Unlike myself, my father is a handsome man, but not a good-looking one. What I mean is that he has a fine head, but he's small and he doesn't have that vaguely athletic air that my tallness and broad shoulders give me. His silver, youthfully wavy hair frames a red face with coal-black eyebrows; his nose is hooked and imperious; his mouth proud and sensual; his light blue eyes have a fixed and almost embarrassing brilliance. My father's is a beauty which, at least for me, is somehow bound up with his professional importance. It's the beauty of a university baron, a well-known and established man of science; in short, it's an irretrievably academic beauty. Why do I say, irretrievably? Because my relationship with my father has suffered from this side to his character, continually and, yes, irretrievably. Right from when I was a child, every time I drew close to him with affection, at a certain point I would feel his professional dignity coming between us, like a transparent yet unbreakable sheet of glass which might, perhaps, permit me to admire him, but not to love him. As a child I never managed to identify the reason for our incapacity to express affection for each other and so ended up attributing it to my own shyness. Later, in adolescence, I put the blame on my father's inability to step out of his public persona; so that bit by bit I found myself almost loathing him. But I have never been sure that deep down it wasn't my fault or at least partly my fault, and not his. But why? What mistakes had I made in my dealings with him? I ask myself this question every morning as I watch him eating, without ever managing to come up with an answer.

My father has finished scraping out the yoghurt carton. Then, very carefully, he pours his coffee and milk into his cup, butters his toast and spreads a thin layer of honey over the butter. In the past, these gestures he makes as he eats were another source of irritation for me: but now that our relationship has changed, I can't help observing that whatever my father does, he does it with perfect control. He eats with measure and apparently without appetite; and when he speaks to me his voice is measured too, soft, benign, and yet beneath it all, in its own subtle way, authoritarian. He asks me what the weather's like, what film I saw yesterday evening with Silvia, where we ate and so on; but I have the impression that he does so out of politeness, without any real interest, or rather, with a curiosity which for some unknown reason he attempts to disguise as casualness and indifference. Finally, with the air of someone who's done his duty, he stops talking and gets on with his breakfast, eyes turned toward the window. So I pick up a paper and settle down to read. I feel I could do with a coffee or a bite of something myself; but despite the fact that my mouth still tastes stale after the night's sleep, I'm determined to hang on with my father until the physiotherapist arrives, which he does, on time, as soon as my father has finished eating.

Small and completely bald, with a thick moustache that seems designed to compensate for his lack of hair, the physiotherapist carries the kind of collapsible black briefcase magicians have. The first thing he does is take off his jacket, exposing shirt-sleeves and braces and thus emphasizing his likeness to a comic character from the silent films of the Twenties. He's talkative, but in a strictly professional, conventionally optimistic and affectionate way. For his part, my father accepts this businesslike cordiality quite readily; he appears to think this is the right and normal way to express his own dependence.

While preparing to massage my father, the physio-therapist, at once cheerful and phoney, exclaims: "Well, Professor, we'll soon be having you up on your feet. Then you can start a new life, Professor, a new life." Equally friendly and phoney, my father replies: "A new life, at seventy, Osvaldo? If anything it'll be a slightly older life."

The physiotherapist then pulls back the bedclothes so that my father's body is uncovered, lying flat and stiff in the middle of his crumpled sheet. My father undoes the knot in the cord holding up his pyjama pants and the physio-therapist, ready to go, pulls them down to his ankles. In the accident my father fractured his femur; the physio-therapist sets to work on the thigh muscles.

How disappointingly different my father's body is from his head! His excessively white stomach with its excessively

9

black hairs seems disproportionately plumper at the top than lower down; his thighs are so skinny and pale they seem to have no muscles at all, and with his legs being so thin, his knees and feet seem too big. But in the white light from a sirocco-blown spring sky, his penis, lying snug in the thick pubic hair above big, bulging testicles, belies the senile appearance of his body. For one thing it's a different colour, darker, with a bronzed look, as if he'd got himself a suntan just there and nowhere else; and then it is unusually thick, as though in a state of permanent semi-erection.

This extraordinary penis made a big impression on me even as a child, because of the highly visible cylindrical bulge that showed where it was in his trousers. Later, I couldn't help sensing a meaningful, though obscure relationship between the size of my father's penis and what I call his academic beauty. Why did I think this? What did the dignity of the professor have to do with the man's splendid genital equipment? And again, why, now, am I unable to take my eyes off my father's penis, why am I inspecting it in something like the same way I was inspecting his face a few moments ago, as if to discover the reason for the change in our relationship after his accident?

I mull over and over these ideas without getting anywhere; meanwhile, still chattering away with his clinical jocularity, the physiotherapist sits down on the edge of the bed and begins an electrical massage of my father's thigh. All at once I have a bizarre idea: seeing as the physiotherapist's massage instrument, something like a vibrator, is going very close to my father's penis, what would happen if he skimmed lightly over it a couple of times? Wouldn't that penis with its sly, sleepy look maybe wake right up, wouldn't it push up into the air, rigid and vertical, despite my father's not wanting it to? This absurd and irreverent reflection tells me it's time I went. I get up, say goodbye to my father and the physiotherapist and hurry out.

Nine a.m. Why do I go and have my coffee down in the bar in the street of a morning instead of sitting at table in the dining room with my father? The thought goes through my head every time I leave the house in the morning, because I'm tempted to have done with this habitual act of protest, the only one left over from the time when, rather absurdly, I took it into my head I would go on living in my father's house, but without spending any time with him and, with any luck, without even seeing him. Of that period, which I feel bound to call heroic, there remains only my ritual refusal to have breakfast, just as, in the body of the whale, one can still find the fossil paw with which in prehistoric times the creature used to drag itself across the *terra firma*. I feel all the while that I ought to have my coffee at home with him – quite apart from anything else, we do keep the same hours – and yet I don't, for all kinds of what, in the end, are fairly obscure reasons. The main one, though, is that in my eyes such a move would amount to a kind of defeat, or rather to the recognition of a defeat. As to what my father thinks of this minimal refusal on my part, I'm not at all sure that he even notices, and this provokes a sense of humiliation: all that trouble simply not to be noticed!

Nine-thirty a.m. Leaving the bar where I ate my croissant and drank my coffee under the puzzled gaze of the barman who doubtless wonders why I don't have breakfast at home, I go back to the block and into the courtyard where I usually park my beaten-up city runabout. Before the accident I would often see my father in the opposite corner climbing into his big Mercedes at the same moment; and each time this happened I couldn't help but feel the same sense of unease you get when you suddenly see your reflection in a distorting mirror. My father, a professor of physics, me, a professor of French literature. Him famous, me obscure. Him happy with his position, me not. Him perfectly integrated, me, to all intents and purposes, alienated. Yes, for me he represented an admonitory mirror where I would look at myself in the hope that I didn't resemble him, and with the fear of discovering, on the contrary, that we did have some features in common. But why this hope, why this fear? Weren't we two completely different people? And most of all, why, now that my father's car is no longer parked in the courtyard next to mine, do I have this feeling almost of loss, of imbalance? Could it be because I exist only in so far as he exists?

In any case, the fact that we both have the same profession has often given me an unaccountable sense of farce, as if of a grotesque coincidence whose meaning, however, escapes me. Before the accident, while I sat opposite him at table during our rather stiff, silent meals together, I would find myself imagining dialogues like this: "Professor, I hate physics." "Professor, I hate French literature." "Professor, I don't like you at all. You're bourgeois, a university baron, a man of the establishment." "And you, Professor, are a failed leftover of the protest movement, a failure as a teacher and a failure in life." Yep, it's pretty difficult living with your own father!

Still, there's no doubt that I am a failure as a teacher. To start with, I don't like teaching, even if I do teach French literature which I know well and love dearly. I don't like teaching because it tires me (there are professors who manage never to get tired by turning their lessons into a routine, but I can't do it) and then because I can't help thinking, as I speak, from the dais, that my students don't understand anything I'm saying, and, what's more, don't care if they understand or not. But there's another, more unusual reason why I don't like teaching: during my lectures I often find myself incapable of controlling my enthusiasm for this or that writer whose work I'm presenting. With the result that I forget I'm talking to my students, who, when I'm in a bad mood I think of as "animals", and let myself go in digressions and interpretations which later, thinking things over calmly, I regret and feel ashamed of, as though I'd opened up my heart to an unworthy audience. But, like I said, I'm not a man of routine. So that the hours I spend teaching are a continual, irritating succession of periods of boredom, when I confine myself to giving information, and then of anger, when I let myself go in my digressions.

One p.m. I come home from the university. Since my father had his accident, I eat with him at a small table set up near his bed. My father eats in bed; he sits up with a couple of pillows to support his back, his plate and cutlery on the bed-trolley. At lunchtime, naturally, Silvia is there too. I say "naturally", precisely because eating with my father is not in fact such a natural thing for Silvia. She doesn't like my father and I know for sure that she would gladly give the occasion a miss. As to why she doesn't like my father, I know and then again I don't know. Certainly it's not for the same reasons I've rebelled against him in the past: Silvia has never had anything to do with the protest movement and the fact that my father is a university baron may even be a plus as far as she is concerned. No, Silvia's motive for not liking my father is something that isn't his fault at all: it's the problem of the flat.

When we got married I found myself faced with a dilemma that was both unexpected and in a sense fatal.

My mother had died when I was a child, leaving me a large flat on the third floor of the block where my father and I were living. During the period of the protest movement, inspired by some strange feeling of polemical altruism, I announced to my father that as far as my inheritance was concerned, I didn't want to know, he could keep the flat himself, I didn't want to own anything. This rejection was inconsistent with the fact that I still lived and had always lived in my father's house. Probably, despite my protest mania, I felt it would be easier to give up something I didn't have, rather than something I did. My father's response on this occasion was typical. He took my announcement with his usual authoritarian benevolence without giving any indication that he was perfectly aware that in the end all I wanted to do was rebel against him. "Okay, whatever you want," he said, "but seeing as you might regret it some day, let's not put anything down on paper just for the moment. You give up your property and I'll go on looking after it in your name." "But I don't want to own anything." "You say that now, but tomorrow you might change your mind." "I don't see myself changing my mind." "That's what you say now, but in the future something might happen that'll make you change your mind." At this point I got annoyed and said nothing more, with the result that I never learnt what, according to my father, was supposed to make me change my mind. Or rather, I didn't find out until I met Silvia. Then I discovered the pretty obvious fact that having a place of your own can be an important asset for a young married couple and, what's more, that it seemed especially important for Silvia, who, until then, God knows why, I had always imagined as sharing my own flexibility and indifference over such matters.

So my father had been right in the end: something was

making me change my mind. Anyone else in my position would simply have admitted that the situation had changed and that, as a result, he wanted to have the flat back. But I couldn't get over this, for me, devastating thought: "In the past, you gave up the flat mainly to deal a moral blow at your father. To go and tell him now that you've changed your mind and want the flat back, would be equivalent to dealing the same blow back at yourself."

In short, by asking my father to give me back the flat, I wouldn't be just any old spoilt kid, who, on getting married, turns to his father for help; no, I'd be that emblematic figure I find the most humiliating of all, the Prodigal Son of the gospels. That's right, my prodigality had been the protest movement and my father, as the story's parabola demands, would celebrate my return by killing the fatted calf in my honour, that is, by giving me back my mother's inheritance. This reflection reminded me of a parody of the parable written by a brilliant French writer: "The prodigal son repents and returns to his father. The fatted calf, knowing his fate, escapes. So to get the fatted calf back, the father kills the prodigal son." In other words, by giving me back the flat, my father would be killing the enemy in me, the rebel.

I mention this bitter joke to explain how I felt at the time and why in the end, after thinking it over for a long while, I decided to live with Silvia in the two rooms my father had offered us in his flat without saying anything to her about the flat that was officially mine. I realize now that not telling her about this muddled affair, where vanity and ideology were rather shabbily mixed up, amounted to lying to her. But at the time I felt that, things being as they were and without a home of our own either inside or outside my father's block, I wasn't so much lying as putting the problem off till the moment came when I'd be able to deal with it. To talk to Silvia about it before then would mean complicating my relationship with her and with my father without achieving any practical results.

In any case, everything went well, or at least for a while I liked to think so. We got married and went to live in my father's two rooms. Very soon, however, I picked up a couple of tiny hints that made me realize that Silvia wasn't happy at all. Then I remembered that when I'd told her that, just on a temporary basis, we'd be going to live in my father's flat, all she'd said was: "To be honest, I'd have preferred to have a place of our own. But it doesn't matter, we'll get on fine with your father. And then, he'll be happy we're staying with him." I don't know why but I asked her what made her think my father wanted us to live with him. With unusual vivacity Silvia replied: "But a blind man could see it, Dodo: because he feels and in fact is, very lonely."

Later on, as I've said, I was forced to think back to that brief remark of hers: "To be honest, I'd have preferred to have a place of our own." In fact, once we'd moved into my father's flat, I realized that Silvia felt hostile to her father-in-law, as if blaming him for the fact that she didn't have a place "of her own". But this supposition, like others of mine, was to remain one of those ideas that never go beyond the realm of private reflection. Silvia never explained the reason behind her hostility and I never asked her to.

I should say at this point that my decision not to insist on knowing more was justified by Silvia's moderation in everything she did and said. Yes, she had said: I'd have preferred to have a place of our own, but she'd said it in a reasonable, submissive voice, which had fooled me. I had thus mistaken for resignation, albeit wistful, what in fact was a point-blank refusal, albeit expressed in the conditional, and sweetly.

Apart from which, there were two other things that prevented me from finding out more about Silvia's unhappiness: the first was that to settle the problem of where we lived I'd have had to face that of my relationship with my father. The second was the car accident which, in a certain sense, justified me in putting everything off until my father had recovered.

And anyway, Silvia didn't show her hostility to my father by being unfriendly, but, on the contrary, by acting with an exaggerated formality that would have fooled anyone but me, who knew that Silvia was not at all given to exaggeration whatever the subject or company. Silvia behaved towards my father like a young daughter-in-law, respectful and attentive, always ready to help. Too ready in fact. Like the times she wouldn't leave the flat if Rita couldn't come for some reason, or would even insist on substituting for her and doing the most unpleasant of chores, such as making up his bed or seeing to his bodily functions.

Two p.m. After lunch, Silvia and I leave my father and go to take our siesta. We walk back down the shadowy corridor lined with shelves stacked with books and into our own bedroom. Here we take off our shoes and stretch out next to each other on the big double bed, not unlike, it occurs to me, a deceased husband and wife lying on our backs in twin tombs. The image is a gloomy one, but it does serve to convey that sense of profound, near sepulchral peace which our bedroom, simply because of its location, inspires in me. It is the most internal and protected room in the flat. Tucked away in a corner of the block with two windows that face inward on a deserted and silent courtyard, connected to the rest of the flat only by the umbilical cord of a long, twisting passageway, this room gives me a sense of security, as if it were a kind of womb where I could always take refuge from life's trials and tribulations. Perhaps it is due to this sense of protected, intimate isolation, which Silvia seems to share, that at a certain point, almost without realizing it, we begin to make love. All at once I draw her body, heavy and yielding, against my own; she lets herself be embraced and embraces me in turn. For a few moments, still dressed, we roll clumsily across the bed, kissing and groping each other with fumbling, impatient hands. Then, as though by silent agreement, we take turns to undress each other. I lift Silvia's pullover up over her arms, she pulls down my fly; I unhook her bra, she pulls down my pants; I slip her skirt off down round her feet, she lifts my shirt over my head. And so on and so forth in a contest of dexterity made clumsy by desire, until we are both naked. At which point our love-making, which so far has been spontaneous and muddled, takes on a sense of order and develops in an almost ritual fashion. I lie flat on my back; Silvia climbs up and straddles me; I lift my hands to caress her breasts, she takes hold of my penis and guides it into her vagina. Then, as she begins to move from right to left and back, swaying gently and insistently with her muscular hips, apparently trying to test the strength of my penis by straining it first to one side then the other, I watch her.

Silvia has an elongated oval of a face with grey eyes that stare short-sightedly; her nose is long and narrow, her mouth small with a sad, sorrowful expression about it. Despite the fact that she's sitting on my crotch, her proud, firm breasts trembling at every movement, her face manages to maintain an expression of contemplative compassion which, ever since we first became lovers, has always given me a sense of *déjà vu*, of something already experienced. When had I come face to face with this expression before? Where had I seen it? Finally, little by little, I managed to remember.

When I was a child my mother used to take me to mass on Sunday in a church not far from our house. It was an ugly, modern church built in a fake Romanesque style with red-brick walls and white stone decorations. Inside, at the end of a nave lined with columns, a huge madonna dressed in white, holding a baby Jesus likewise in white, stood out against the sparkling new gold mosaic of the apse. I knew and understood nothing of the mass, and although I liked the ritual of the gestures and the splendour of the vestments, I felt it went on too long and would get bored. On the other hand I never grew tired of looking at the enormous madonna who, haloed head lightly inclined to one shoulder, stared down at me in an attitude of inexplicable compassion. Why did the madonna feel sorry for me? I didn't ask myself the question so straightforwardly, but deep down it was the reason behind my amazed and dreamy contemplation. Why then, I wondered, in that kind of thought without words typical of a child's mind, did the madonna feel sorry for me: I was a happy child, I had everything I needed, I was healthy, I lived with my mother and father, I even had a governess, everybody loved me, or at least so it seemed . . .

Now, every time I make love with Silvia, lying on my back beneath her, watching her from below as her big breasts loom over me and her hips work hard to bring me to orgasm, the resemblance of her face, and above all her expression, to the face and expression of the Byzantine madonna of my childhood, fascinates me and intensifies my pleasure, bringing to it a symbolism I can't quite place. Thus Silvia, for as long as our love-making lasts, becomes an emblematic figure strangely superimposed over a real person, she is a woman who works my penis hard and, at the end, watches me as it empties in orgasm, yet at the same time she is the madonna who understands all things, forgives all things.

This near religious contemplation of mine lasts almost to the very end and is matched by a similar contemplation on Silvia's part. Then I can't hold off any more; I contract and writhe in an orgasm where pleasure and pain vie for the upper hand and, in closing my eyes, I'm dimly aware of the blasphemous analogy with the way one lowers one's eyelids at the elevation of the host. At this point the identification of Silvia with the madonna vanishes as she now has the orgasm she's been holding back, waiting for mine. Her crotch ceases to shift from side to side, back and forth; instead it makes a series of violent jerks like some kind of machine gone mad, and then she throws herself down on me, her mouth searching for mine. A long embrace punctuated by repeated spasms follows this perpendicular fall of the madonna, only a moment ago so compassionate and so distant. Finally, Silvia tears herself from my arms, jumps down from the bed and disappears into the bathroom, but not fast enough to stop me catching a glimpse, through the shadows, of a typical young woman naked with broad shoulders, slim waist and generous hips. Perhaps she senses that to my eyes she is no longer the madonna to be watched from below with chaste devotion, but an ordinary woman who runs off to the bathroom after sex, her hand held between her legs to stop the sperm from dribbling. More than once, in fact, getting out of bed, she has insisted: "Please, don't look at me."

Three p.m. I go out for my early afternoon walk. This is my favourite time to walk because the traffic isn't too heavy and there aren't many people about. I get my car out of the courtyard and drive along the Tiber down Lungotevere della Vittoria, not far from Piazza Mazzini in the Prati part of town. At a certain point the road along the river is closed due to a subsidence of the bank; they've been working on a new embankment for quite a few years now, but in the meantime traffic is prohibited and they've put up a red-and-white striped barrier across the road. Shaded by the leafy fronds of the big plane trees, free from traffic, its tar all cracked and full of weeds, the riverside road beyond the barrier is an excellent place to take a walk. But after parking my car, the first thing I do is to go and lean on the parapet over the river and look straight ahead. This gives me a view of a broad avenue of acacia trees and, above the houses in the distance beyond, the dome of St Peter's. I'm not an architecture enthusiast; if I look at the dome it's for a special reason that has nothing to do with art. I look at it, in fact, to check whether a certain something does or does not happen. As a rule, nothing happens. But some-times, when the weather is stormy and the sky is a shifting pattern of thunderclouds and great rents of blue, all of a sudden I get the impression that from behind the dome there sprouts, grows, rises, swells and finally towers that well-known mushroom-shaped cloud of the nuclear ex-plosion. I am perfectly aware that this cloud isn't and can't be the result of an explosion. I tell myself I must be the victim of a hallucination arising from some casual re-semblance; but all the same I do feel a kind of gloomy pleasure in gazing at the dome and fantasizing its de-struction. My contemplation of the basilica, which I im-agine as having collapsed in the midst of a panorama of rubble, lasts for as long as it takes the cloud, blown by the wind, to lose its mushroom shape. Then, having once again established that I've simply imagined seeing what wasn't actually there, I resume my walk on the other side of the barrier.

Five p.m. I go home. Silvia is out on her own and I'm in two minds whether to sit with my father or go to my study and read or listen to music or maybe even mark my students' essays. Like Silvia, I'm convinced that not only is my father very lonely but that he finds loneliness difficult to cope with. I deduce this from the ill-disguised pleasure with which he usually greets my arrival in his study. "Oh, it's you," he says quite superfluously, and immediately stops reading the book or paper he has in his hands. But sometimes my father has other visitors right around five o'clock and then I realize with a slight but inevitable sense of disappointment, that he doesn't so much like my company as fear being left alone. You or somebody else, you can imagine him thinking, it's all the same to me; best of all though, somebody else female. Yes, because my father often gets visits from women, generally mature or even older women, women who, intuition tells me, have all been his mistresses in different periods of his life. There are a couple of teachers, two or three middle-aged, upper-class ladies, an ex-student, still young, a mature countess and an old princess. My father has apparently kept up his relationships with all these women and, in fact, they treat him with affection, devotion and admiration. What's more, I suspect that during their visits since the accident, two or three of them have indulged in the occasional fleeting sexual contact. But whatever the truth of the matter, if I knock at his door and find him in the company of one of these women, he has an almost ironic way of introducing me, without inviting me to sit down, and then maybe adding, "He's a professor like me," which has me leaving as soon as possible with a feeling, I can't deny it, of renewed dislike.

As a result, I generally go off to the other end of the flat, to my study: this is next to our bedroom and like the bedroom has an arched ceiling, white walls and a single window looking out over the courtyard. What do I do in this silent, secluded, monastic room? I put some classical music on low, sit awkwardly on a stool in front of a small desk and mark my students' essays. At a certain point, without having a fixed timetable, just going on the mood of the moment, I put the essays away and start to read, still sitting at my desk. Sometimes, though less often, I take off my shoes, throw myself on the bed and begin to day-dream. I don't daydream about the end of the world; that very abstract fantasy I reserve for when I wake up of a morning. No, I daydream about literature, mainly French literature. What I sometimes find myself doing in a fragmentary way and almost in spite of myself during my lessons at the university, I now do on my own, in complete freedom and without any feelings of self-reproach. I weave literary theories around something I've recently read, or I think of a fictional character as if he were a real person, or of a writer who really existed as if he were a fictional charac-ter. In the end I doze off to sleep.

Eight p.m. After a short, heavy sleep of fifteen minutes or half an hour, I wake with a start and immediately think of Silvia. Since we have an agreement that she goes out on her own in the afternoon, I'm never quite sure whether she's in or not. All the same I start looking for her with a feeling of terror almost, as though I were afraid she might have left me. First I go into the bedroom and sometimes I find her there: she's just arrived and is getting changed. If she's not in the bedroom, I look for her all over the flat: in the kitchen, in the dining room, in the sitting room, in my father's study, in the bathroom even. Oddly, she's never where I think she's going to be. If I look for her in the bedroom, she's in the study, if I look for her in the study, she's in the sitting room. If she's here I find the large room in almost complete darkness except for the corner where she's sitting, all alone and as though in distress, waiting for me with a book in her hand. Invariably she says: "I felt tired, I didn't feel like talking, so I sat down here to read.

Anyway, Rita's sitting with your father." She sounds apologetic, as if excusing herself for not having done, this once, her duty as an affectionate and devoted daughter-in-law. Finally, more rarely, I sometimes find her in my father's room, sitting in the armchair at the bottom of the bed, silent and detached, intent on watching TV with him. Then I can't help noticing, and I find this rather sad, the evident relief, joy almost, with which she greets my arrival, jumping to her feet and immediately asking if it's already time to go out to eat.

Nine o'clock. We say goodbye to my father who has his dinner with the nurse, and go out. As a rule we eat in restaurants, though sometimes we may go to friends' places, always Silvia's friends. At this point I should explain that my social life, if we can call it that, which was meagre enough before 'sixty-eight, more or less ceased to exist when the protest movement ended. The few friends I used to spend my evenings with either went underground or left Rome altogether, some of them to go abroad.

Silvia's position is different. Not being interested in politics, she has never broken off her at once affectionate and superficial relationship with a certain kind of bourgeois middle-class group that I call "papist", since it seems to me they were already around in Rome before the Unification with precisely the same mentality and precisely the same interests. "If we all went back a century and a half," I jokingly say to her sometimes, "your relatives and friends wouldn't have any trouble adapting, they'd find themselves perfectly at home." She agrees with me; she accepts that they're narrow-minded, boring people, but then, rather mysteriously, she goes on seeing them just the same, organizing dinners in their houses or trips and picnics in the country or by the sea, or then again evenings at the opera or in concert halls, with the reasonable justification that "you have to do something", you can't live "in isolation".

The evenings I like best are the ones when we eat alone in a Chinese restaurant that's just a short walk from our block, in a square in the old part of town. It's a reasonably cheap restaurant and the food isn't terribly good, but the place does have that truly oriental quality of being quiet in a way that is somehow furtive, something entirely lacking in the rowdy trattorias of Rome. We sit at a black-and-red lacquered table, our backs to a screen decorated with patterns of almond trees in bloom and herons in flight. Over our heads hang coloured lanterns made from tissue paper; from the kitchen come whispers and muted sounds; every time the door opens the repetitive tinkle of a carillon rings out. I sit opposite Silvia and gorge myself on rice, beanshoots and chicken, listening to her and simply agreeing with inarticulate sounds and nods of the head. What does Silvia talk about? Nothing, now I come to think of it. But this nothing, made up of tiny observations, confidences, reflections and comments, finally develops into that atmosphere that usually goes under the name of intimacy. A discreet, reasonable, domestic intimacy which resembles Silvia herself. Sometimes I feel Silvia isn't saying anything because, really, everything between us has already been said. But when? Here's another mystery; if I think about it and ask myself the question seriously, I have to admit, never. So what's involved would seem to be a purely physical intimacy created not by the meaning of the words at all, but by the tone of voice and the glances and gestures that accompany the words.

Ten p.m. After dinner, as I said before, we often go to the cinema. Once we've taken our seats in the dark, Silvia puts her hand in mine and we watch the film holding hands, just like a regular husband and wife should when they're doing something that brings them together. Sometimes, if we haven't made love in the early afternoon, Silvia, who appears to think that no day should go by without sex, begins, after a while, to feel me up. She does it without my asking or wanting her to. In the dark the hand on my knee frees its fingers from my own, creeps towards the tab of my zip, pulls it down in little tugs and slips in between my pants and my stomach. Then, without hurrying, little by little, under cover of a coat thrown over my legs, she gently but insistently frees my genitals. She begins to stroke slowly and thoughtfully and seems quite deliberately to break off every time the pleasure becomes too intense, picking up again as soon as it's got back to something bearable. It's a knowing and, in its own special way, ruthless kind of stroking; sometimes I find myself comparing it to those tortures based on the systematic alternation of pain and relief, the Spanish garrotte method, for example, which, like Silvia's stroking, is dragged out as long as possible, alternating periods of strangulation with periods of breathing. Finally, perhaps afraid I'll have my orgasm before the moment she's decided on, Silvia bends down abruptly and finishes with her mouth what she began with her hand. At this point, while her head is going up and down over my groin with an impatient, near furious action, I can't help but wonder what it is that inspires in her such a single-minded determination to have me ejaculate. The first thing that occurs to me is that it won't always be like this: Silvia and I still love each other as much as we did when we were just married, more so probably; but this love, heightened as it is by sexual passion, won't last for ever; so Silvia is simply trying to make the best of our love while it lasts, the way people try to make the best of a sunny day shortly before winter. But I also sense that this thirst for sex she has is partly due to an unconscious aspiration to maternity, that is to the need, again unconscious, to make quite sure that when the time comes the aspiration could be promptly satisfied. The notion of a maternal instinct constantly lying in wait may perhaps be confirmed by the fact that after my orgasm Silvia doesn't get rid of the sperm by spitting it out into a handkerchief, but swallows it with a solemn, symbolic hunger, as if aware that at that moment her mouth is substituting for the womb which presides over conception.

Midnight. Our return home, after the cinema, marks the end of my day. A typical day in my life at thirty-five, with me doing more or less the same things I did every day a year ago and that, barring the unexpected, I'll probably still be doing in a year's time.

But one's day-to-day existence with its repetitions and habits runs parallel to the drama which, when there is one (and there often is), seems totally devoid of any connection with that humdrum life. One cleans one's teeth, goes to the lavatory, eats one's meals and goes to sleep, day in day out, even when one's future, or that of an empire, is in the balance. Thus in choosing to describe my everyday existence, I didn't mean to imply that there is no drama. On the contrary, it was with just that in mind that I have tried here and there in this account of my habits to hint at the cracks that may sooner or later become irreparable rifts. One of these threatening cracks recently appeared in the structure of my marriage, which I have so far described as a relationship of reassuring stability and happy monotony. One morning, Silvia left. She packed the few things she couldn't do without in a suitcase and left a note saying that at least for the time being she wanted to go and stay with her aunt. This didn't mean she was leaving me for good; just that she wanted to "reflect" on her life. In fact she added that she would like to see me at least once a week at our regular Chinese restaurant not far from the flat.

CHAPTER TWO

The Pale Pink Seashell

Of the many literary theories which, during my lectures, I find myself giving away off-the-cuff to my obtuse and apathetic students with a generosity I later regret and feel ashamed of, there is one that has recently taken shape in my mind with suspiciously neat precision: this is voyeurism, that seems to lie at the source of a great deal of fiction writing and, obviously, of cinema too. On the other hand, voyeurism does not seem to be present in painting or sculpture, since these arts have no movement – the voyeur doesn't fasten on the subject, so much as on its movement, or behaviour. What's more, this behaviour must be strictly private, that is, it must be such that no one, except a voyeur, could chance to see it without being aware that he is guilty of an indiscretion. In other words, and restricting myself to written narrative, as well as having us see what anyone could see, the novelist often has us see what no one could see, unless of course they happen to be a voyeur. And in fact, while one can hardly attribute the representation of happenings as public as dance festivals or parliamentary sittings to the writer's voyeurism, the representation of an event as private as sexual intercourse is quite definitely voyeuristic. And this for the very good reason that people don't make love in public and that hence, when the novelist describes two characters in the act of union, he is, in effect, watching, and having us watch, through an imaginary keyhole. This voyeurism of the narrator is often mirrored by the voyeurism of a character in the book, as happens, for example, in the well-known scene in Proust, where Monsieur de Charlus is watched by the narrator while making love with the *giletier*, Jupien. Or, again in Proust, there is the equally well-known scene where Mademoiselle de Vinteuil is seen making love with a girlfriend.

But the voyeuristic scene par excellence is the one in Herodotus where the queen is spied on while undressing both by King Candaule's favourite and by the king himself. This scene is doubly voyeuristic because the king is watching the favourite while he watches the queen. What's more, in Herodotus's story, the voyeurism doesn't function as a pretext, as it does in the Proust, but constitutes the story's theme.

And I could go on; but I chose to mention Herodotus and Proust if for no other reason than to demonstrate that voyeurism runs through the whole history of narrative, from its origins to the present day. Enough of examples though. Instead I'd like to explain how my own improvised literary theory came about. So, I started thinking of voyeurism as a narrative source after reading not a novel at all, but a poem by an author I've recently been presenting to my students: Mallarmé. It's a poem that takes its title from the opening line: "A negress possessed by the devil".

Here it is:

A negress possessed by the devil
Wants to taste a little girl saddened by the new
And evil fruits underneath her tattered dress;
This glutton contrives some cunning tricks.

Against her belly she rubs two blithe young breasts
And, higher than hand could grab,
She thrusts the dark shock of her booted feet,
Just like some tongue unskilled in pleasure.

Against the frightened nudity of this gazelle
That trembles, like a mad elephant, flat
On her back, she waits, eagerly admiring herself,
Smiling childish teeth at the child.

And, between her thighs where the victim stretches,
Lifting open the black skin beneath the hair,
She pushes out the palate of that strange mouth,
Pale and pink as a seashell.

The poem belongs to that genre normally referred to as obscene. It describes, or rather narrates (since the scene is in movement), the erotic position usually known as the sixty-nine – with the triple peculiarity that it is a sixty-nine between two women, it is a sixty-nine between an adult and a child, it is a sixty-nine between a black and a white.

But what interests me most of all is not the obscenity, but the voyeurism, which is twofold: Mallarmé not only has us look in on something as strictly private as a scene of lesbian love, but also something private within that privacy, that is the inside of the female sex, usually hidden from view by the pubic hair. You can watch a nude woman through a keyhole for as long as you like, but you won't see what nature didn't intend you to see, unless, as in Mallarmé's poem, you watch her "in movement", in action. So I would say that what we have in this poem is a voyeurism intensified by a kind of profane curiosity. Because to force one's gaze beyond the confines established by nature is an act of profanity, is it not?

Voyeurism, as I've already pointed out, begins with the observation of the movement of the object watched. This is precisely the case with the object of our gaze in Mallarmé's poem. But first of all, what is the situation and who are the characters both watched and watching? First and foremost there's the negress, the black woman: just for once she is not the victim but the torturer. The victim on this occasion is white and, what's more, a young girl with barely budded breasts and an immature body; but a girl already corrupted, already initiated into the world of erotic games. Corrupted, but not yet hardened: in fact she trembles with emotion as she pushes her head between the spread legs of her seductress to hazard the very intimate caress that has been asked of her. But the little girl isn't just corrupt and frightened, she is also poor. Her dress has holes in it, through which one can glimpse the immature lines of her prepubescent body. In contrast with the girl, the black woman, animal, laughing and sure of herself, acts as though in a position of social superiority. The black woman is enjoying herself, the girl suffers and obeys.

So how did this encounter between two such different characters come about? If we imagine the scene as taking place in Paris at the turn of the century, when, without doubt, there were already African women in the city working as housemaids and cleaners etc., then we can assume that the black woman is a cook, or maid, and the girl a beggar or messenger. The black woman has had her eye on her victim for quite a while; one day, in the sleepy early afternoon, she approaches her with the prospect of a present, or even, more frankly, with the promise of earning some money.

The seduction scene takes place in the kitchen where the black woman has first of all satisfied the little girl's hunger. Then, having got her shy and fearful consent, she takes the girl by the hand and has her climb the five floors up the back stairs almost at a run.

They arrive at the attic with its sloping roof and little window looking out over the roofs of Paris. "Possessed by the devil", the black woman forgets to shut the door properly; she throws herself on the bed, spreads her legs, and points the child imperiously to her sex. Hesitant, embarrassed, fascinated, the little girl lifts her rag of a dress off over her head, approaches the bed and starts to climb up. The black woman helps her, sets her down, turns her round and pushes her head down between her thighs; at the same time, she thrusts her belly up against the girl's small breasts and lifts her feet into the air, still clad in the boots that in her hurry she hasn't bothered to take off. The child, or rather victim, as Mallarmé calls her, is now trembling with fear: all the same she stretches herself between her seductress's legs and hazards the first caress. Meanwhile, poking her head out to one side, the black woman watches, or rather spies on the girl, and laughs with childish gratification.

Now we come to the voyeur. It's not difficult to imagine him as the son of the master of the house, a boy without sexual experience, but curious. The way the scene is presented supports this view. He happens to be, and perhaps it's no accident, on the top floor where the servants live, and going down the corridor he hears talk and laughter coming from behind a door left ajar. So he approaches, pushes the door open a little further and looks in. The first and only thing the boy sees is "the palate of that strange mouth, pale and pink as a seashell". That is, at that very moment he discovers not only how the female sex is made, but how it behaves in action too. And yet, as the boy realizes, this discovery has something profane about it, because what he sees spread open before his eyes is something nature intended should remain closed, hidden, invisible, unknowable, and hence, in a way, sacred. To look at it is to violate its sacredness. Yet the boy doesn't turn away and doesn't close the door: rather he stares all the harder, justifying himself with the notion that this is a discovery. Basically, the boy accepts his own voyeurism with the reflection that by watching he is broadening and deepening his knowledge.

Let's concentrate a while on this discovery-aspect of voyeurism. The voyeur spies not only on what is forbidden, but also on what is unknown. In other words, voyeurism implies a need to discover the unknown. And all at once it comes to me that there's an obscure, but unquestionable relationship between the way voyeurism discovers things and the way science does. Because the scientist who manages to discover one of nature's secrets through the extremely narrow crack of a daring experiment, must, whatever people say, experience the same feelings of burning curiosity and profane challenge that the inexperienced boy of Mallarmé's poem feels when he sees the incredible apparition of the "pale pink seashell" through the crack of the door.

So? So the gaze of Mallarmé's boy has the same profane character as the gaze of the scientist when confronted, for example, with the composition of matter. As for the scientist's feelings towards his discoveries, feelings of burning and ultimately sacrilegious curiosity, there can be no doubt: all the descriptions we have of the state of mind of research-workers during their experiments confirm it. But at this point I'm struck by the analogy between the words "fission" and "fissure", or "crack". The scientific process which led to the discovery of atomic energy implies an initial split or crack – words that can equally well be applied to the female sex as to the atom. In both cases there is the discovery (in the literal sense of uncovering an object hitherto covered) of one of nature's solemn mysteries: the mystery that since time immemorial has cloaked both the composition of matter and the origins of life.

But doesn't such an analogy between two discoveries so different in both intent and consequence risk being arbitrary and unjust? Isn't there, in short, a substantial difference between the curiosity of the voyeur and that of the scientist? I consider this objection and decide that it's well-founded. But so be it: one doesn't think only so as to think of things that are just; one also thinks, and often one thinks especially so as to think of things that are unjust, but that one can't help thinking about.

With this in mind, I park my car near the barrier that marks the beginning of the stretch of riverside road closed to traffic and go and lean against the parapet at the exact spot that gives you a view of the dome of St Peter's. I have a Polaroid camera slung around my neck. I want to photograph the cloud that sometimes gives me the mistaken but irresistible impression of an atomic mushroom rising into the sky from behind the basilica. I want to see if there is indeed a casual likeness or whether I'm hallucinating.

The weather is right for the experiment. It's a spring day, windy and stormy, the blue sky crossed in every direction by big white clouds. Mechanically repeating the words "fission", "fissure", "crack" to myself like some obsessive, sarcastic refrain, I focus the polaroid and wait.

And, yes, along comes a cloud to the right of the dome, gradually swelling and changing shape in the wind. But it is still a spring-time cloud, crazy and cheerful, its belly swollen with rain, edges tinged gold in the sun. Then, all at once, the cloud takes on a threatening look. A moment ago it was a capricious continent of soft, luminous cotton-wool. Now, no doubt about it, it's a gigantic mushroom, dark with poison, its stem rooted in the ground while the head above spreads wider and wider, grows darker and darker. The cloud of a moment ago made one think of a prose poem by Baudelaire: "So what do you love, extraordinary stranger? I love the clouds, the clouds that pass ... Over there, over there, the marvellous clouds." But the mushroom-shaped cloud that I now think I'm seeing would be better described by a quotation from the *Bhagavad Gita* which the physicist Oppenheimer is supposed to have muttered on seeing the blinding light of the nuclear explosion illuminate the desert of New Mexico: "I am death that carries all away, overthrower of worlds."

But I'm here to photograph the cloud. So, after looking long and hard at the dome and the cloud, way down at the end of the avenue of acacia trees, I snap the shutter. The print pops out almost immediately, like a mocking tongue. I wait, shaking it in the air to let the images dry and at the same time following the cloud's continuing transformations in the sky. Shoved and pitched about by the wind, it has lost its mushroom shape now. Like the cloud that Hamlet points out to Polonius it could be anything: a camel, a weasel, a whale, whatever. In short, it goes back to being a harmless, cheerful spring cloud and nothing more. So, at last I look at the photograph. Ambiguous as Hamlet's cloud, the image seems to suggest my capacity for hallucination more than anything else. It's me who sees the bomb everywhere. And trying to photograph it to demonstrate its existence or otherwise doesn't help at all. I slip the photograph in my pocket and set off on my walk again.

I reach the red-and-white barrier and push on along the

ruined tar, full of blisters and cracks, where the river road has subsided. There's no one walking by the parapet and no one on the pavement by the houses. Then I do something new: as a rule I walk along by the parapet, watching the river which makes a picturesque curve at this point; but this time, I don't know why, I start walking on the pavement opposite, by a row of small apartment buildings whose first-floor windows are at eye-level. Then, leaning out of one of those windows, I see somebody I've seen quite a few times before, a black woman, probably a maid with some family or other.

I slow my pace to get a better look at her. She's leaning forward, at a right angle, her breasts pressed against the windowsill. The black of her arms, bare to the elbows, contrasts sharply with the white of her angora pullover. She's young and round her head she has the same ring of short thick curls you sometimes see round the foreheads of Roman statues. The nose is small and wide with open nostrils, the mouth set in a capricious, ironic expression. Her bright, round eyes are staring at me hard.

It's immediately clear that she's watching me. And it's equally clear, it seems to me, that I switched pavements to see her better, or perhaps even to talk to her. And in fact, as I arrive under her window, I say quite naturally "Good afternoon."

She replies by wishing me the same in French. The voice is sweet but cold. I pick up the conversation, speaking French myself. "It's not such a nice afternoon actually."

She immediately rejects the conventional dialogue and attacks me in a near passionate tone of protest: "I've seen you hundreds of times, you always go by in the early afternoon, it's as though you were an old acquaintance by now. But why don't you ever look at me, why do you always walk along with your head down, why don't you notice me, what's wrong?"

I'm embarrassed and reply in a jokey, evasive way with a phrase from the prose poem by Baudelaire I quoted before: "I'm out for fun, to relax. I don't look at anything, at most I look at the clouds."

She starts to laugh, showing off a magnificent set of teeth: "Better look at a woman than at the clouds."

So, I can't help thinking, amused, I quoted Baudelaire, and she, without realizing it, echoed Mallarmé's poem about the black woman. "Are you from Senegal?" I ask her.

She smiles and, as if playing a childish game, answers quickly and happily: "No, guess where I'm from."

"From the Ivory Coast?"

"No, I'm not from the Ivory Coast."

"Mali?"

"Wrong again."

At this point I seem to have exhausted my meagre knowledge of French-speaking Africa. Smiling, I say: "I really don't know where you're from, Africa's so big."

In her sing-song voice, she agrees: "Yes, Africa is big. I come from the biggest country in Africa. From a country that's changed its name."

Finally I get it. "From the Congo."

"Which is now called Zaire," she corrects punctiliously.

I don't know what to say next. Watching her, I'm fascinated by an unusual feature of her body. Although she has the bust of a normally shapely woman, behind, bent over the windowsill, I can see the butt of a different and altogether more substantial figure. I'm so distracted by this disproportion between bust and backside that I don't say anything for quite a while, searching through my memory for the right epithet to describe the phenomenon. Finally, I have it: "callipygous".

She says: "I don't suppose you could tell me what you're thinking about?"

I hesitate, then decide to tell the truth: "I wasn't thinking about anything. I was looking."

"And what were you looking at?"

"At your behind."

She starts laughing, reaches a hand behind and gives herself a slap on the buttocks: "Big, isn't it? It didn't used to be like that, not until three years ago. It went and grew on me unfortunately."

"Why unfortunately?"

"I was a model. I had to give up because of it."

I change the subject. "Do you live alone though, or . . ."

"I live with a man called John. He plays the drums."

"And he's from Zaire too?"

"No, he's American, from Virginia."

I'd like to ask her if he's black too. With remarkable intuition she interrupts, laughing brightly: "John is white, whiter than you, with blue eyes and blond hair."

So, I think, she's found a way of letting me know she lives with a white. "And where is John now?" I ask.

"He's on tour in Sicily."

"And what are you doing here all on your own?"

"I'm not on my own, there are some other girls. We play cards, watch TV. When I'm alone I stand at the window and watch the people going by."

"Nobody ever goes by here."

"You do."

I tell myself that this is a pretty direct way of letting me know she likes me. And at the same time the disturbing and somehow superstitious thought comes back that she might be Mallarmé's negress "possessed by the devil" and placed there at the window by a strange, erotic-literary providence.

I ask: "What's your name?"

"Pascasie."

"Well, Pascasie, right when I spoke to you, I was thinking of an African woman."

With a spark of jealousy, she immediately asks: "An African woman you love?"

"Not exactly. But she did make me think of love, yes. Let's say, she's a woman I like."

"More than me?"

The question is serious; she's not smiling now.

I hesitate: "In a different way."

"Where is this African woman?"

I'm suddenly struck by the absurdity of this conversation, on Mallarmé, in the street, between pavement and window. "Look," I suggest, "your John is away on tour. Let me come up if you want to talk some more. Otherwise I'd better be getting on with my walk."

With unexpected wariness, she says: "But I don't even know who you are."

I quickly introduce myself: "My name's Edoardo, I'm a professor of French literature. But you can call me Dodo, like my wife does."

"What a strange name. In French, to go 'dodo' means to sleep."

"Dodo was also the name of a race of birds that went extinct. I belong to a race that's going extinct too."

The word race makes her suspicious: "Aren't you Italian?"

"Of course I'm Italian, but I'm also an intellectual, an animal that's dying out, that is."

She watches me with growing suspicion. Finally she sighs: "I don't know if I'm doing the right thing letting you come up. John's a jealous type, and then I don't know you."

"So come down, we can walk and talk. I'll take your photograph if you want."

I mentioned the Polaroid by chance, but immediately realize that I've pronounced the magic word that opens every door. She says quickly: "No, no, you come up, let's take the photo in the house."

Without a word I move to the gate. She shouts: "I'll go and open up," and disappears.

I cross the garden and go into the entrance hall. Pascasie is already there, standing at the door to her flat in white trousers and a white pullover. With her black face and arms she takes on the weird, spectral look of a photograph in negative. Stiffly, as if from a distance, she offers me a long, thin, cold hand, then turns her back on me abruptly and goes ahead into the flat. I then get confirmation of what I've already glimpsed from the street. Pascasie seems to be a combination of two different bodies: from the waist up she's a young woman with a regular shape; from the waist down the extraordinary volume of the buttocks reminds me of Mallarmé's "mad elephant". But one has to admit that she does move with a light, graceful gait, so that the callipygous aspect of her body is far less obvious now she's walking than when she was leaning out of the window.

The sitting room has that typical rented-accommodation furniture, Swedish style. Pascasie invites me to sit down on a skimpy sofa with a green cover and varnished black legs. She sits on a narrow little chair, her powerful hips sticking over the edge. Not without some difficulty she crosses her thighs in an attitude appropriate to social conversation. I look around: incongruously, some African masks, obviously fake, have been hung above the Swedish furniture. Spread over one wall is a set of photographs, all of Pascasie in different clothes and poses. In one colour photo she's not alone: she's arm-in-arm with a young man, dressed in the bizarre way drummers do dress: yellow shirt, purple sash, green trousers. It's John, obviously. I can tell from the mop of curly blond hair. Pascasie picks up our conversation at exactly the point which seems to interest her most: the existence of an African woman in my life.

"So, you're in love with an African woman?"

I answer ambiguously: "I don't know if I'm in love. And then, how can you be in love with a ghost?"

She pulls a solemn face. "Oh, is she dead?"

"No, she's alive, very alive in fact."

"And where is she?"

"In a book."

Once again she looks at me suspiciously. "In a book? I don't understand. You love this African, so she exists. But if she's in a book, she doesn't exist, she's made of words."

"You can love someone made of words too, can't you, a fictional character?"

"What's the name of this character?"

I don't know why, but I answer quickly, "She's called Pascasie."

"Like me."

"Yes, like you. In fact, come to think of it, you are the character."

She starts to laugh. "Me? A character in a book? But I'm a woman made of flesh and blood. Touch me, here and here, and then tell me if these are words."

So saying, she takes my hand and, despite my reluctance, pulls it to press against her arm and then thigh. "You call these words?"

I withdraw my hand. "Obviously they're not words, but you do look like the woman in the book. It's as if you'd come straight off the page."

She asks, serious: "What's the book? A novel?"

"No, it's a book of poetry."

"By an African poet?"

"No, French."

"A good poet."

"I'd say so, yes."

"Recite me the poem."

I fall silent a moment, embarrassed. I hadn't expected this request. "I don't have the book here with me, and I don't know the poem by heart."

"But what does this poet say about the African woman?"

"He says she looks like an elephant."

Offended, she protests: "There you are, those are the kind of things whites say about blacks. An African poet would never have said such a thing about a woman from his own country."

"Elephants are beautiful too," I say calmly.

"What else does he say?"

"He says she has beautiful teeth."

She laughs on purpose to display two rows of close-set, brilliantly white teeth. "My teeth are beautiful too. And then?"

"He says she's cheerful, naive and that she laughs."

"Doesn't he say anything else?"

I'm silent for a moment.

"He says she's possessed by the devil."

"By the devil?"

"Yes, by a demon, a spirit, you know."

She becomes thoughtful. "Where I come from, the women possessed by spirits are witch-doctors. And what does the spirit make her do?"

"It makes her make love."

She starts to laugh: "You don't have to be a witch-doctor to make love."

"She doesn't make love with a man."

Another laugh. "Oh, with a woman. And to think, I

42

don't understand it, but those sort of women are always after me. There's one who sends me flowers sometimes."

"Not with a woman, with a girl."

She isn't taken aback in the least, but I notice that although she's still laughing, her eyes have suddenly grown serious, with a gleam of cold curiosity. Then, quite suddenly, it dawns on me that she's watching me, spying on me in fact. It's as if, at the very moment Mallarmé's negress pulled the girl on top of her, she were also keeping an eye on the voyeur watching the scene through the crack of the unclosed door, voyeuristically contemplating his excitement as he does hers. In short, anything you can do I can do better. So even if I were to spy on Pascasie, I wouldn't be the voyeur at all; the voyeur would be Pascasie herself, spying on me spying on her.

And in fact she goes on: "How do the black woman and the girl make love?"

"They do the sixty-nine."

"What's that mean?"

I tell her brutally: "Everybody knows what that means, and so do you."

She's quiet a moment, but not in the least unsettled; then she laughs: "Oh, and so? But you're not telling me the whole story. You've got something in mind, an idea, it's obvious."

"What?"

She's still laughing. "An idea you got from the poem about the black woman. Perhaps you've been thinking about it for a while. Then you saw me, at the window, made up your mind and started talking to me, acting on this plan you've got."

"But what plan?"

"If you hadn't had a plan, you wouldn't have brought your camera. Oh, Dodo, you know what you are?"

I'm at once pleased with myself for guessing what Pascasie thinks of me, and at the same time irritated because the idea is hardly flattering. I ask: "So, what am I in your opinion?"

As I expected, her answer agrees perfectly with my intuition. "A voyeur, a little voyeur who goes around with his Polaroid and would like to take photographs of a black woman making love with a little girl. Oh Dodo, Dodo, I always thought there was something strange about you when I used to watch you walk by, something special. Now I'm sure of it."

Oddly enough, although she's still laughing, her eyes, deep down, remain serious, cold and almost hostile. I wonder what kind of hostility it is. The hostility of black against white? Or of the uneducated against the educated? Or the proletarian against the bourgeois? Or woman against man? Or all these things together?

To gain time, I say: "But I didn't write the poem about the black woman."

"No, but you'd like to photograph me making love with a girl."

Her eyes are probing my reactions. They shift back and forth across my face like the beams of a searchlight across a dark stretch of country. Then it comes back to me that, thanks to my earlier intuition, I have the knife, so to speak, by the handle: it's not me who wants to do the watching, to take the photographs, it's she who wants to watch me as I watch and photograph.

I say harshly: "I only asked to take a photo of you on the street. It was you invited me in."

I wait a moment, then add with fake carelessness: "Would you mind being photographed though?"

She starts to laugh: obviously she thinks I've already put my foot in the trap: "You see, you are a voyeur!" Then,

44

getting serious again, she explains: "Well, listen: no sixty-nines with little girls, or women either, or even men. But if you want to take photos of me on my own, with or without clothes I've got nothing against it. I used to be a model. It's my job. Obviously you'll have to pay me for the session."

"How do you want me to photograph you?"

Once again, at the back of her coal-black pupils that insidious coldness appears: "Like the African woman in your poem, if you want."

"She's naked, but with ankle-boots."

"I've only got boots. What are these ankle-boots like?"

"The kind they used to wear a century back, with buttons, or laces."

"I haven't got any like that. If you want I'll put my boots on. But how does she pose with her boots, the woman in the poem?"

"She's got her legs apart."

"And then he says he's not a voyeur!"

"I didn't say I wanted to photograph you with your legs apart. I merely told you that the African woman in the poem has her legs apart."

So we go on sparring around her and my own voyeurism, while in reality the question was already settled before we began: because for every voyeur there's an exhibitionist, and for every exhibitionist a voyeur. Finally I say: "Where do you want me to photograph you, here, or somewhere else?"

"Let's go in the other room."

She gets up and goes ahead of me, small-breasted, but plump and round behind; her small, regal head, crowned with curls, stands erect on a round, strong neck. We go into the bedroom where the double bed is so big it takes up almost the whole floor, leaving just a narrow space each side to move about. Pascasie goes to the head of the bed and starts to undress slowly, one piece of clothing at a time, watching me as she does so with cold, wary eyes, as if trying to see what effect she's having on me. Standing up at the other side of the bed, I put on a show of composure and lack of curiosity, pretending to examine my Polaroid.

Pascasie pulls down her trousers; for a moment I have the impression that under these white trousers she has another, black pair. The triangle of her pubic hair is a different black, less luminous, strangely small and under-sized. She starts to move around the room; under the deep inward curve at the small of the back, the abundance of her buttocks creates the impression that she's leaning forward a little as she walks.

She goes to a wall-cupboard, opens it and takes out a pair of boots.

I gesture for her to stop: "No, no boots."

She turns, a shade disappointed: "How do you want to photograph me?"

"I'll do you like Manet's 'Olympia': Manet was a contemporary of the poet who wrote the poem about the African woman. There's an African in Manet's painting too, Olympia's maid, holding a bunch of flowers to her breasts. But I'll put you in Olympia's place."

"Who was Olympia?"

"A beautiful white woman."

Without a word, she climbs on the bed and stretches out in the pose of a Venus by Titian. Her small breasts and prominent belly add to her Renaissance look. She looks at me and again I see that cold, prying curiosity typical of the voyeur. The truth is that while exhibiting herself she's searching me for any possible excitement aroused by her exhibition. Suddenly I ask: "Why are you watching me?"

"It's you that's watching me, isn't it?"

"So let's say we're both watching each other."

46

She burst out laughing: "You're right. But how do you want me to pose?"

"Like Olympia, hang on, I'll arrange you myself."

I go over to her and discreetly arrange her body in the pose of Manet's Olympia, half-leaning on the pillows, one arm crooked with the hand on her lap. Jokingly I say: "Now all we need is a white maid behind you with a bunch of flowers."

"But didn't your African woman have her legs apart?"

So saying, she makes as if to shift her legs, and I realize that, just so as to catch me out, she'd be quite capable of exhibiting herself, of showing me Mallarmé's "pale pink seashell", even though I don't want her to. The thought doesn't tempt me in any physical way. But in an intellectual way, yes. To photograph Pascasie in the pose of Mallarmé's negress would amount to translating my theory on voyeurism in art into practice. Unfortunately, however, we would both be naked at the end, she in the flesh and I in the spirit.

I say drily: "Forget the poem. I'm going on Manet's painting now."

She seems unhappy, but says nothing. I lift the Polaroid, focus and squeeze the shutter. Then I take out the print and begin to wave it in the air, telling her: "That's enough, I don't need any more."

She looks at me, doesn't seem entirely convinced, and says: "Dodo, at a certain point you changed your mind, why?"

I feel I owe her an explanation. "I didn't change my mind. Perhaps for a moment I did mean to photograph you in the same pose as the African woman in the poem; but it had to be a photograph taken exactly like any other photograph of any other object. I don't know, a glass, a rose, an apple. Instead I realized that you were intending to watch me while I photographed you. In other words, you wanted to amuse yourself at my expense with the spectacle of my, let's say, curiosity. So the best thing to do is to forget the whole thing."

Pascasie looks at me as if trying to get a good grasp of what I said. Then it's clear she's understood because she breaks out in a delighted, slightly false laugh: "Oh, but how intelligent you are Dodo. You're a terrible voyeur, that's for sure, but really, I mean really intelligent with it, and I have a big soft spot for intelligent men."

I say nothing. I pull my wallet from my pocket, take out a banknote and lay it on the bedside table. Still laughing, Pascasie takes the note and gives it back to me: "This wasn't a session, you only took one snap. Here, take your money, give me a kiss instead and don't say any more about it: you're curious about me and I'm curious about you."

With an effort I free myself from her impetuous hug and say: "At least accept the photograph then."

"Ah ha! You're afraid your wife will find it on you."

With unexpected bitterness I say: "My wife isn't the jealous kind."

"And you?"

"I am."

"I'm happy to have met you, you know. Will you come and see me again?"

"Yes, sure, some day or other."

I find myself on the pavement by the Tiber again with a sensation of relief. Like in the past, at school, after a tough exam you only just managed to pass.

48

CHAPTER THREE

Destiny's Jokes

～∽～

I'm at the Chinese restaurant, waiting for Silvia. This is the third time we'll have seen each other since she, as I can't help but describe it, ran away, though she denies having run away and even I can't imagine what could have made her do so. By now the first violent impulse to know the truth has faded in the face of Silvia's sweet but obstinate evasiveness. I have accepted that it's going to take a long time to understand whatever lay behind her decision to leave home and "reflect on the situation".

Thus my relationship with my wife has become a little like the relationship between a prosecutor and a mysteriously reticent witness. Everything else, even love, now seems to depend on my success in this quest for some sort of truth. I say "some sort" because probably there's not just one truth but a number of equivalent interchangeable truths. In the meantime though, I have rejected Silvia's somewhat cynical proposal that we make love at her aunt's place when her aunt isn't there. Silvia was amazed by my refusal and asked me with a strange sadness if I didn't love her any more. I replied that, on the contrary, I loved her more than ever, which was precisely why I didn't want to make love before I'd sorted out the mystery of why she ran away. To which she replied, with a shrug of the shoulders, that there was no mystery and that she hadn't run away.

But here she is. She pushes the door and comes in, setting off the long tinkling of the bell mechanism. She walks casually between the tables, heading toward me. She really does look the calm, worry-free woman coming to an appointment with an old friend who can be kept waiting. She's about twenty minutes late in fact and excuses herself with an air at once breathless and careless. I watch her as she sits down. She's wearing a leather jacket with a fur collar which makes her look awkward and plumper than she is. But above the collar her slim neck rises gracefully to the elongated oval of her face. I think, as so often in the past, that the grey staring eyes, the nose with its narrow nostrils and the mouth set in an expression of sorrow, give her the look of a primitive madonna, and the spontaneous recurrence of this comparison cheers me up, showing, as it does, that nothing has changed between us, that I still love her with the same love – that love which, during sex, when she's on top of me, mercilessly tormenting me with the powerful, imperceptible movement of her hips, has me looking up at her with devotion, the way you look at a sacred image. So? Will I be able, in spite of my unchanged love, to be cold and perceptive in my quest for the truth, whatever that may be? But Silvia is slipping off her jacket now. She hangs it on her chair, puts on her glasses and studies the menu. Suddenly unable to control myself, I dive straight in: "Listen Silvia, you and I have got to talk today."

She raises her eyes from the menu, surprised: "But we've

always talked; every time we've been here we haven't done anything but talk.''

I correct her: ''I didn't explain myself very well. By talk, I mean, talk about your running away.''

''But I didn't run away. And then we've already talked about my, what shall we say, change of residence. I've already told you: imagine I've gone away to stay with my relatives in Grosseto for a while.''

I get heated all of a sudden: ''It's not the same thing and you know that as well as I do.''

Silvia chooses her favourite dish on the menu, chicken with almonds, and gives her order to the waiter. Then she takes off her glasses and stares at me a moment with short-sighted, vaguely questioning eyes: ''Okay, let's talk, what do you want to say?''

''I'm convinced that what's behind your so-called change of residence is, logically enough, the problem of the flat.''

As if taken by surprise, she immediately repeats: ''The problem of the flat. What problem?''

Impatiently, I say: ''You said it yourself: the problem of not having a place of our own.''

She answers slowly and firmly: ''The problem of finding a place of our own has got nothing to do with what you call my running away but which actually is merely a result of my wanting to think things over.''

''Think what over?''

''My life.''

''Couldn't you think it over at home, without going away?''

''No, I want to think my life over away from home, without you.''

''What's so special about your life that you have to leave home?''

''Nothing.''

"So why didn't you stay?"

"Oh God, Dodo, why do you make me repeat everything? I didn't stay because I needed to think my life over on my own."

"On your own?"

"Yes."

"Perhaps you don't realize," I object, "but certain things do operate on an unconscious level. The truth is that this miserable business of the flat is coming between us, putting a greater and greater distance between us."

She replies with a careless bluntness: "I really don't think so. I even said we could make love at my aunt's place when she's at the office."

"But I want to make love in my own home."

"No, that's out."

"But why?"

"Because then I might as well come back to your place, don't you think?"

"You see, the real reason for the crisis in our relationship is the problem of where we live!"

"But Dodo, how can one not want to have a house of one's own? What kind of family is it that doesn't have a home of its own? But that doesn't mean that when I left that morning it was because of the flat."

"So, you're asking me to believe that there's another reason behind your running away?"

"I didn't run away, please, for the nth time of asking, don't use that expression. I told you: I want to be on my own and think."

She's quiet for a moment, then adds: "But *you* don't come into this thinking at all."

"Thanks."

She reaches a hand across the table and says: "Don't be a baby, now."

The contact with her hand inevitably rouses my emotions. "But do you love me?" I ask her.

She says nothing and gazes at me with such sorrowful compassion that I haven't the courage to insist on an answer and restrict myself to looking at her hand. It's a beautiful hand, different from her body, more like her face, long, tapered, smooth with a tentative spirituality about it, as if frightened of itself. I watch her with the attention of the naturalist who has picked up a large starfish on the beach and now examines it as the creature just barely moves the tips of its arms, instinctively seeking the deep water where it was swimming only a short while ago. With the same at once thoughtful and instinctive vitality, Silvia's long delicate fingers lie spread on the table as though, without Silvia's realizing it, they were arranging themselves in the most graceful way possible. I think of this same, so spiritual hand when it circles my penis in the ring of thumb and index finger, not squeezing too hard, barely touching in fact, just gently shifting the angle of erection before taking it in her mouth. And then I tell myself that the contrast between the spirituality of the fingers and their erotic performance is nothing but an illusion; that probably they have neither spirituality nor eroticism but just a single, unconscious vitality capable of expressing itself simultaneously in both ways. From here to a clarification of Silvia's ambiguity toward me is only a small step: yes, she is the primitive madonna and the insatiable lover both at the same time, and never either the one or the other alone.

Following this train of thought I finally say with an effort: "Do you know what the word destiny means?"

"Everybody knows, don't they?"

"What do you think destiny is?"

"Oh God, Dodo, what do you take me for? Destiny is . . . destiny."

"That is?"

She thinks it over, then says: "Something that comes from outside, that doesn't depend on us and that draws us in. War, for example."

"Good. Now listen a minute. The protest movement begins, 'sixty-eight, and I let myself – it's your own definition, and a good one – get drawn in. Destiny!"

"Why destiny? You *chose* to be drawn in."

"Wait a moment, in my case 'sixty-eight is only half of the destiny aspect. The other half is you: I meet you, I fall in love with you, and at this point destiny is complete."

"In what sense?"

"Because in 'sixty-eight I did something that, fifteen years later when we got married, I was bound to regret."

"And what was that?"

"I owned a flat in our block. To protest against my father and everything he stood for in my mind, I gave up the flat and left it to him. In short, I failed to foresee you and your hankering for a place of your own. Destiny!"

She looks at me surprised: "You never told me about this flat, you always said you didn't own anything."

"It's true, since 'sixty-eight I haven't owned anything."

"How come you had this flat?"

"My mother left it to me."

Silvia says quickly: "There's just one thing I don't understand. Seeing as you were rebelling against your father and that to rebel you left him the flat, why did you go on living with him?"

I find it difficult to explain to Silvia that I stayed with my father precisely because I was opposed to him. Sometimes hate is quite as clinging as love. Head down, I say: "I don't know. Probably the fact that I'm forced to depend on him is also part of my destiny."

I fall silent a moment, then go on: "What comes out of

all this pretty clearly is that, for good or ill, I had chosen a certain way of life, and then you came along and the whole thing went to pieces. In other words, I find myself faced with two equally reasonable but contradictory demands: it's reasonable for you to want a place of your own: but it's also reasonable that I should want to remain faithful to certain principles."

"Principles or resentments?"

"Principles *and* resentments."

After a moment Silvia says: "I don't see any contradiction between the desire to live in one's own house and what you call your principles, but which I think are resentments. No, it's a simple problem that you can settle in a simple way."

"How?"

"By asking your father to give you back the flat."

"No, out of the question."

"But why?"

"It would be like admitting I'd been beaten."

"Beaten? But who by?"

"By my father, or rather, by everything he represents."

"But he wouldn't think that at all. He loves you. He'd just think that you needed the flat, that's all."

"Who cares what he'd think! What matters is what I'd think."

Silvia is quiet, then says with unexpected, exasperating objectivity: "Look, I think you're right. Seeing as you dislike your father so much, you shouldn't ask him to help you. It would mean losing self-respect."

"You see! And yet you won't give up the idea of having a place of your own. Isn't that what I've been calling destiny?"

She looks at me quite a while and says finally: "I'm not saying that destiny doesn't come into it. But I can assure you that there is no relationship whatsoever between the problem of where we live and the fact that I went away."

We watch each other. I have the sudden, disconcerting impression that I'm chasing a butterfly which flutters about, then lands, then right when I'm on the point of grabbing it, flies off again. Without thinking, I say: "So, all I can imagine is that you left because of my father."

She looks at me surprised: 'What's your father got to do with it?"

"You can't stand him, you don't want to live with him."

She shakes her head: "Quite the contrary. In some ways I find your father fascinating. Apart from anything else, I was his student. I knew him before I knew you. It's you, not me, who can't stand him."

We watch each other. Silvia continues softly: "Dodo, believe me: I haven't got anything against your father, nothing."

I accept: "If that's the truth, there's only one explanation left."

"Which is?"

"That you don't love me any more, that you went away to avoid physical contact with me."

"But I said we could make love at my aunt's place!"

"You knew I'd refuse."

She ignores this.

"Anything else?"

The almost bureaucratic tone of her question infuriates me. I look at her with an acute sense of frustration and it suddenly occurs to me that it isn't so much a butterfly as my whole life that's eluding me. With a change of tone, I say: "You don't want to tell me why you left. So why the hell do you come here? Why do we go on seeing each other?"

I realize that I'm raising my voice in the hush of the almost empty restaurant. Silvia watches me without saying a word, but this time her look of contemplative pity exasperates me: "So, do you want to talk, or don't you?"

As I speak, I pick up the light porcelain plate decorated with big golden flowers and bang it down sharply on the lacquered table-top with both hands. The plate breaks in two perfect halves, leaving me holding one in my left hand, one in my right. At the same moment the waiter arrives with our food, imagines I've broken the plate to protest about the slow service and begins to apologize profusely. Upon which things get chaotic: the waiter apologizes; Silvia, bewildered but determined, gets up and heads for the door; beside myself and desperate, I run after her.

Silvia walks out of the restaurant. We're both standing on the pavement in a blustery spring wind that blows in our faces and seems indistinguishable from our suffering.

I shout: "Silvia, you can't do this to me," and grab her arm.

At the touch of her round, strong arm, I feel an enormous desire for her, a desire all the stronger because I'm sure she's about to pull away from my grip. But she doesn't. Instead she turns, gazes at me without anger, then says softly: "If you go on like this, you really won't see me any more."

"Let's go back in, for God's sake."

So we go back in and are received by a bowing restaurant manager who, like the waiter, doubtless believes that Silvia rushed out to protest, as I had, against the service. We sit down, the waiter takes away the broken plate and we begin to eat in silence, working away with our chopsticks, heads down.

Then I lay down my chopsticks and say: "Perhaps the flat problem isn't the reason why you ran away. But I'll act as if it were. So I promise that from today on I'll do my best to get you a place of your own. Is that okay?"

I watch her insistently. She says nothing. Then she picks up a lump of rice with her chopsticks, looks at it and says slowly: "It's not okay, but it doesn't matter. Most of all, let's not say any more about it."

CHAPTER FOUR

Father and Son

For some time now my father's old nurse, Rita, has been replaced by her niece, Fausta. It was Rita who specifically recommended Fausta and although she isn't really a nurse my father, now on the road to recovery, seems happy with her. Coming home this morning, having picked up the papers at the kiosk in the street, I find the kitchen dark and deserted. Fausta isn't there. So I sit down by the window and wait.

A short while later Fausta comes in carrying a bag with some cartons of yoghurt for my father. She says, "Good morning," a bit brusquely, puts the yoghurts in the fridge and sets about lighting the gas ring. "Is Father awake?" I ask.

"You bet he is!" she answers.

From her brusque gestures and snappy tone I realize I'm supposed to ask her why she's in a bad mood. So, without giving much sign of being interested, I ask: "What do you mean, 'You bet he is'?"

"I mean he's more than awake."

"Can one be more than awake?"

"You bet you can!"

For a moment I don't say anything, watching her. Perhaps because Fausta has so far restricted herself to getting on with her work in a meticulously conscientious fashion without showing any sign of getting personally involved, the allusive scorn of her answers has me looking at her as if I were seeing her for the first time. She's small, but perfectly proportioned, so that, albeit on a miniature scale, you could say she was shapely. With her hair cut very short, her head looks like a boy's, or rather, thanks to an indefinably shifty, ambiguous look she has, like a callow young hooligan's. She has dark eyes, gentle and sly, a short, almost snubbed nose and a fleshy mouth set in an expression of challenge. Her red sweater swells over her chest, tracing the outline of two pert breasts; her jeans are tight to bursting round the twin cheeks of her backside; a red heart-shape has been stitched onto the left buttock and she has a yellow kerchief knotted round her neck. "Listen, Fausta," I finally put it to her, "are you going to tell me what you've got against my father this morning, or not?"

In an eloquent piece of pantomime, she pretends to be absorbed in her contemplation of the coffee-pot heating on the burner: "I know what."

"So tell me."

"Too complicated, forget it."

She turns her back on me and talks to the gas ring. I decide to resort to the direct method: I get up from the table, go up to her, take her by the shoulders, swivel her round and tell her forcefully, right to her face: "Now will you do me a favour and tell me what's got into you without wasting any more time?"

To my surprise, she doesn't wait to be asked twice this

time, perhaps because I firmed my question up by using the *tu* form.

Calm and fluent, she says: "You remember before, when my Aunt Rita was here, a male nurse used to come at half past eight to give your father his morning wash and clean and then leave at half past nine. Your father was in a lot of pain and he needed a nurse just to clean him up. This went on even after I took over from my aunt. Then, one fine day, your father changed everything. He sent the male nurse away and decided that I should clean him up from now on. Why do you think he did that?"

"Probably," I tell her, embarrassed, "because he felt better and didn't need the male nurse any more."

"But," she corrects me, "the agreement with me was that I didn't have to clean him, only to help him during the day. I warned him right from the start that I didn't want to clean him up, and when I say clean up, I don't just mean sponging him down, shaving him and changing his pyjamas, I mean the bedpan and all the rest too."

I object: "But your aunt used to do it for him sometimes and you took her place."

"My aunt did it for him because he didn't ask my aunt for anything else."

I begin to understand but pretend not to: "What else could he have asked her for?"

"Look," she answers, being reasonable, "maybe I would have agreed to clean him up and so on. But he didn't go and get rid of the male nurse and ask me to wash him, shave him, change his pyjamas and maybe even take him the bedpan because I'm his nurse, but because I'm . . . well, because I'm me."

This time I can't pretend not to understand any more because Fausta tips me a sly wink. "Oh," I say, "it's like that, is it?"

"Yes, it's like that."

She doesn't say anything for a minute; then, taking the now boiling coffee-pot from the burner and beginning to lay the yoghurt, butter and honey on a tray, she adds: "You go ahead and take him his breakfast now. Then I'll come and give him his injection and I'd like you to watch carefully what happens."

"What happens with what?"

"Let's call it, the injection trick."

"But what trick?"

She turns to face me again: "Haven't you realized that whenever I come for the injection or have to clean him up, he asks you to go out? And why do you imagine he wants you to go? Obvious, to be alone with me. You do get me, right?"

Fausta's allusions are getting on my nerves: "No," I say, "I don't get anything at all."

"What does a nurse do when she's cleaning somebody up, or before an injection? She rubs the patient's body with her hands, or she helps him undress. With her hands again, right? Now, he wants those hands to go somewhere where there's really no need for them to go. Now do you get me?"

I say firmly: "Aren't you capable of telling him to leave off?"

She shrugs her shoulders: "It's like talking to the deaf. Once, twice, okay. But he never gives up. One moment it's the injection, the next washing, then at night there's his glass of water. Even when my hands are busy with the bedpan he has a go."

I feel humiliated by these complaints; and at the same time humiliated by the fact that I feel humiliated. In a bored, cold voice, I say: "I'm sorry, but if you want to leave, all you have to do is say so. We can look for another nurse."

To my surprise, she shakes her head. Then says with unexpected sweetness: "No, I don't want to leave. I just wanted you to know."

"And why's that?"

"Because. Just to let you know. You're always hurrying off, you don't even look at me. I wanted you to realize that I'm doing my best for your father."

Spoken with pretended embarrassment, her words remind me of other, similar words. Whose? Ah yes, it was Pascasie, the African woman, when she was leaning out of the window over the road by the river. "You hurry by," she said. "You never look at me." So it seems, I tell myself – and in doing so I feel less humiliated, less the son of an unworthy father – it seems it's impossible for a man to get on with his business without arousing the ever watchful curiosity of women. I lower my eyes to Fausta's hand as she places slices of toast one by one onto a plate. It's an abnormally large hand for such a small person, smooth and fleshy with slightly puffy fingers ending in thick oval nails varnished in a dark red that verges on black. One thing's for sure, I think: these aren't the inevitably work-worn hands of the professional nurse.

"How old are you?" I ask.

"Twenty-two."

"How long have you been working as a nurse?"

She looks at me with fake-sincere confusion: "To tell the truth, this is the first time. Or rather, I was nurse to my uncle, Aunt Rita's husband, for two years. He's lost the use of his legs too, like your father. Except that your father will get better whereas with my uncle it's permanent. So when Aunt Rita suggested I take her place, I accepted, because by then I felt I was good at the job."

"And what did you do before working as a nurse?"

"I worked for my fiancé for a couple of years – a photographer. I helped him. We lived together and we were going to be married. But then we broke up and seeing as I didn't want to go back to my father's, I went to stay with Aunt Rita and she taught me how to be a nurse."

The tray is ready now. I stand and pick it up. But Fausta stops me. "Look though, you must promise you won't say anything to your father."

"Why should I say anything to him?"

"It's just that, he is a great man, and one has to forgive him his weaknesses. And then, I've got to like him now and I wouldn't want him to be upset."

Unexpectedly, and disconcertingly, a light of genuine, heart-felt kindness shines through her eyes.

Surprised, I tell her: "Don't worry, I won't say anything."

But she wants to use the secret she has told to get on more intimate terms with me. She goes on: "I've told your father lots of times: if it makes you happy, maybe I'll do it. But you must understand that I don't feel anything at all for you, really nothing."

Intrigued, I can't help asking: "And what does he say?"

She shrugs her shoulders: "Oh, he doesn't care what I feel. He just wants that, and that's the end of it."

"So he doesn't take it badly when you tell him you don't want to?"

"He never takes anything badly. He's sweet, kind, affectionate as a father. But beneath it all he's stubborn. He knows what he wants and he wants to get it whatever it takes. He thinks I'll change my mind."

I say quickly: "Right, I understand, but now I really must take him his breakfast."

I take the tray and go to the door. In a tone of complicity she reminds me: "I'll be coming for the injection in a few minutes then."

This time I don't answer, but slip out into the corridor. As often happens when I walk along the twisting intestine that links the two ends of the flat, I feel a faint but lucid sense of angst. Do I feel like this because until recently the corridor constituted a concrete expression of our, mine and

Silvia's, dependence on my father; that is, of the fact that we didn't have a place of our own? Or is it because the bookshelves that line it remind me of my father's past? Rather than "past", I should say culture, if the word didn't seem so inappropriate for this collection of tired old books thrown together with no more order than that of my father's occasional reading which has always followed the fashions and issues of the day. I don't mean his scientific books of course: my father keeps those carefully ordered and what's more specially bound in the big Empire-style bookshelf behind the desk in his study. No, I'm talking about the miscellany of reading material, or rather – given his eclectic tastes – entertainment material, which has caught his attention at one moment or another over the years. There are some once famous, now forgotten novels, the obligatory classics, and then various works of philosophy and history. On one shelf the enormous tomes of two now out-of-date encyclopaedias are stacked in a row; another is full of old art books, large and small. One thing you can be sure of is that all these books date back at least twenty years. I couldn't say why but it seems that at a certain point in his life my father stopped reading for curiosity and relaxation and concentrated entirely on his specialist publications. Or rather, he would buy certain, I suppose you might say, inevitable authors: Proust, for example (the complete works), just to have them around and perhaps with the intention of reading them in a future that has never materialized. Every time I walk down the corridor, I notice, not without a sense of cruel satisfaction, that these now yellowing books are still unopened, unread. Alas, my father's mind was young once, but today those books testify to his old age.

The door to his room is ajar and I push it open with my foot. Supported by two cushions, my father is sitting up in bed, shaved and combed in freshly-ironed blue pyjamas with lighter cuffs and lapels. Seeing him so scrubbed and spruced up like this, I can't help thinking of Fausta and her accusations. How many times, during the cleaning process of a short while ago, did my father try to coax some kind of erotic attention out of her? My father returns my greeting without turning round. He's looking out of the window over the roofs of Rome, apparently watching something interesting. All at once he turns and says: "Got it."

Pushing the trolley to the bed, I ask: "What are you talking about?"

"About a ginger cat that was stalking a poor sparrow. Right when you came in he made a leap and caught it. What patience though! I must have been watching him for a quarter of an hour."

My father has a stern face and gentle voice. His white and now rather long hair has a silvery shine and frames a red, a darkish red, face. Thick coal-black eyebrows shadow his light-blue eyes. His nose is hooked and imperious, his mouth full and proud. But beneath this energetic and relatively youthful face, his age comes out in the folds and stretch-marks on the skin of the neck.

I ask: "What did the doctor say yesterday evening?"

"He said I should try and walk."

"And so?"

"So one day soon the physiotherapist will bring me some crutches and I'll have a go at walking."

His tone is despondent and ironic. The trolley with the breakfast tray is at his chest now. My father pours some coffee, then takes the yoghurt carton, pulls off the lid and begins to eat. I watch him and ask myself if I hate him. I'm convinced that if you hate someone, you hate them most when they're eating, because eating is a supremely selfish act arising out of the most pressing of necessities. But no, I don't hate him, I can't manage to hate him. He's too well mannered and, as we all know, even the Christian spirit begins with good manners. There's no doubt that my father derives enjoyment from the fresh, acidy taste of the yoghurt, the fatty, delicate taste of the butter and the sweet, sharp taste of the honey, but it's clear that he doesn't want his pleasure to show. No, this isn't a man eating; this is a university professor partaking of the required nourishment, discreetly, calmly, with detachment. So, no hate in me for him then; just reflections on the difficulty of hating him.

My father has finished. He gives a light push to the trolley, picks up one of the papers and opens it up. But there must be something bothering him, something that prevents him from concentrating on his reading, because all at once he asks: "Aren't you going to the university today?"

As often happens when one has a deep-seated worry, I say something I hadn't planned to say but that was obviously preying on my mind, urging me to speak: "My lesson is later today. I'll take the opportunity to stay with you a while."

"Thanks."

Why do I want to take the opportunity presented by having a later lesson to stay with my father? I wasn't thinking of staying with him a moment ago, nor had any desire to do so. I go on improvising: "Don't thank me. I've got a reason for staying that may annoy you: I want to talk to you."

"Talk to me? What about?"

Meanwhile, I've finally realized what I do want to talk to him about. It's obvious. I want to talk to him about Silvia and her craving to have a house of her own. I answer ambiguously: "About something that, for me at least, is very important."

This time he turns his head and looks at me. Then, with unexpected paternal benevolence, he says: "If it's important for you, then it must be important for me too. So, what is it?"

I'm suddenly overcome by an insurmountable feeling of

shyness. I'm never shy when I'm sure I'm right; but I am when I'm not sure. And this is precisely what's happening to me now. The fact that for the last fifteen years I've based my life on a rejection of everything that, in my opinion, my father stands for, means that by coming to him now to resolve my personal crisis I seem hopelessly in the wrong. For fifteen years I have dreamed of living in a spirit of rejection and renunciation; and here I am waking up from my dream with the intention of accepting everything I rejected and renounced.

Amidst these thoughts, or rather, amidst these unwelcome, paralysing feelings, my eye falls on the book my father has on his bed. It's a book on the effects of nuclear war, one I almost forced on him a few days ago. He said he didn't want to read it, he wasn't interested. In the middle of this overwhelming attack of shyness, it suddenly occurs to me that the question of the nuclear threat is almost as important to me now as the reasons behind Silvia's running away. Immensely relieved at having found such a natural escape route, I ask: "Have you started the book, then?"

A little surprised, my father glances vaguely at it, then says: "To tell the truth, not yet. So, what's this important thing you want to talk to me about?"

With an embarrassed gesture I point to the book: "That's what I want to talk about."

"But I just told you, I haven't started it yet."

"Not exactly about the book itself, but the nuclear issue. I want to ask you a few questions."

Was my father afraid I wanted to talk to him about something else? Perhaps. He certainly seems relieved. In a benevolent tone, he says: "Finally. You didn't talk to me about these things all those years when I was still interested in them. And now I've left all that stuff behind me, you start getting curious."

I say: "I don't want to ask you for scientific information. My questions have to do with the – how can I put it? – human aspects."

"Human?"

"Yes, I mean with the people who carried out the experiments, the ones we have to thank for bringing us nuclear weapons."

My direct, personalized way of tackling the subject surprises my father who was obviously expecting a different approach. Jokily aggressive, he says: "What have you got against these people? There's not much can be said about them. They were all good men who believed in what they were doing and did what they believed in."

"I've no doubt that they were, as you say, good people," I say cautiously. "What interests me is whether, despite the fact that they were such different individuals (who, for example, could be more different than Fermi and Oppenheimer?), they nevertheless had a trait in common."

"I should say so; they were all scientists."

"I'm not talking about their profession," I correct him. "I mean a psychological trait."

My father opens his paper again, using the gesture, perhaps, to have me appreciate that although he's not withdrawing from the conversation, the subject doesn't interest him. Glancing through the headlines, he says distractedly: "What trait?"

"I don't know what to call it. Curiosity would be too weak, indiscretion inaccurate, profanity too strong. Let's say, pure, burning curiosity."

"Why burning?"

"Because it's like a devouring fire, inextinguishable, destructive."

My father clarifies: "You were speaking about curiosity, but what curiosity?"

"The curiosity that lies behind the experiments."

My father finally puts down his paper and asks: "Why call it curiosity? Why not call it thirst for knowledge, for example?"

"Because thirst for knowledge is a figurative expression of a rhetorical kind. Thirst is a physical sensation; we use the word thirst to indicate an urgent need: our body uses thirst to warn us it can't survive without a certain amount of water. We can perfectly well survive, on the other hand, without . . . let's say, without looking through a keyhole at a couple making love."

Of course, when I come out with this phrase, I'm thinking of Mallarmé, of the imaginary boy from a good family staring at the "pale pink seashell" through the crack of a door left ajar.

But for my father, who doesn't know what I've been reading, the comparison must seem eccentric to say the least. He frowns: "What have keyholes got to do with it?"

"This. They define a type of curiosity that we can call libidinous."

It doesn't take my father long to realize what I'm getting at. In a strangely altered voice, he exclaims: "So, in your opinion, the people who did the research on splitting the atom had the same kind of curiosity as somebody who squints through a keyhole at a couple making love?"

I start to laugh, happy that he's understood: "Deep down, very deep down, yes."

"They weren't curious," he retorts, convinced, "they were analysts."

"But curious all the same."

He says wearily: "I really don't understand what you're driving at."

"Nothing. I simply want to say that when it reaches a certain level of excitement, curiosity is always indicative of

69

derangement and blindness. The curious man is a common man, very common. And precisely the fact that he is curious demonstrates that."

He yawns ostentatiously to show he's had enough: "Next you'll be discovering that curiosity is the mother of science."

I hit back ferociously at the objection: "Of course, right, it's a cliché, but in this case, long live clichés."

My father says nothing, disgruntled.

I add more seriously: "I want to stress the fact that those people you call analysts were common, I mean mediocre, exactly because they were 'just' analysts."

"Huh!"

"So much so that they hadn't foreseen the effects of their own curiosity, they were surprised by their own discoveries. You know what Fermi said about splitting the atom?"

My father doesn't reply. It is clear that the insistent tone of my voice is bothering him enormously. I quote deliberately: "God, with his inscrutable designs, made us blind to the phenomenon of atomic fission."

My father gives a slight shrug of the shoulders: "I've never heard that one. Where did you read it?"

"In that very book you've got there on the bed."

"What are you shouting for? I'm not deaf."

"Sorry. All I wanted to say was that the analysts were no more than regular curious people."

Under his breath, but loud enough to be heard, my father comments: "Oh, come on!"

"Because otherwise they would have foreseen the long-term effects of their discoveries. The curious person doesn't think of the future, he lives in the present, or rather in the very moment in which he indulges his curiosity."

My father says nothing and this time his silence is definitive. I realize that I've nothing left to say about splitting the atom, whereas everything remains to be said about Silvia and her desire to have a place of her own. Still, talking about the atomic question has served to get me over my shyness. But how to change the subject now from this to Silvia?

I have the same sense of helplessness you get when, having set off at great speed along a motorway, you don't know where the exit is to get off again. How can I tag the question of Silvia onto that of the atomic bomb?

Then I have an idea, I think I've found the exit, the link. It's a pretext, it's true, and almost indecent, but it is a real link. Raising my voice, and with fake indignation, I say: "These analysts, these curious scientists, didn't foresee the effects of their discoveries. I wouldn't have said all that about curiosity if I didn't feel personally harmed. Hasn't it ever occurred to you that I might want to have children? But how can you bring children into the world if you know in advance that they're destined to become, as a recent expression so neatly coined it, 'radiation fodder'?"

Of course I'm lying through my teeth. Neither I nor Silvia want to have children. I stop a moment, then go on: "And as I see it, my case is more than common, it's pretty nigh universal. The nuclear threat doesn't hang over just one or two countries, it threatens the whole of humanity. So you tell me: if, as seems evident, the experiments of your so-called analysts haven't got anything to do with the good of that humanity of which I am a modest representative, then what have they got to do with?"

"With the unknown."

Was it he who spoke, or someone else? I see him put on his spectacles and pick up his paper again. I realize that I'll have to hurry up and get off the subject of the bomb. Now that I've mentioned Silvia, I know where to find the exit. In a doubtful voice I repeat, "The unknown?"

"Yes, that which is not as yet common knowledge, which we don't know about, and which, as a result, is unknown."

My father speaks through clenched teeth, impatiently from behind his paper. Obviously he wants me to get out of his hair as soon as possible. So – to stay with our metaphor – my hand forced by the urgency of the situation, instead of leaving the motorway at the exit, I simply drive over the central reservation.

"Dad, I wasn't telling the truth a few moments ago. It wasn't the problem of the bomb I wanted to talk to you about, it's something else, something personal, private."

My father lowers his paper and echoes, parrot-like: "Personal? Private?"

"Yes, it's about Silvia."

My father's expression suddenly changes from the bored seriousness of the expert obliged to argue with the ignoramus, to that, I don't know whether genuine or fake, of the affectionate father: "Ah, Silvia. What's new with Silvia?"

"I saw her again yesterday. We've agreed to get back together."

Without showing the least surprise, apparently indifferent, he says: "I'm glad to hear it. To tell the truth, I could never understand why she left."

By now, for better or worse, I'm over the central reservation and there's nothing for it but to head off down the opposite carriageway: "There was a reason and Silvia has never kept it from me, but I made the mistake of not taking her seriously. Silvia wanted a place that, as she puts it, would be 'of her own'."

After a short silence, I add: "Of course, you mustn't see this desire of hers as a criticism of you or of the fact that we live with you. Silvia likes you and has got nothing against being here. It's just that, as I said, she wants a place of her own."

A lightly ironic expression crosses my father's face: "A very feminine desire."

"Right."

With pointed politeness, he asks: "And what are you thinking of doing to satisfy this desire?"

I had always thought that going back on my so-called life commitment made in 'sixty-eight would be pathetic, painful, humiliating. But no. With the maximum spontaneity, along comes the contrite prodigal son to take the place of the angry protester. Almost without thinking, I say: "Dad, you remember of course that some years ago I told you I wanted to renounce what I inherited from Mother. You told me the inheritance mainly consisted of a flat in our block. Now, given that Silvia wants to have a place of her own, I'm asking you please – if you'll forgive me the word-play – to renounce my renunciation. I mean, to return the flat to me."

While I was speaking I was all the time aware that I was expressing myself in an unnatural, embarrassed way. Renounce my renunciation! What a complicated and stupidly facetious way of saying, "Give me my flat back!"

But my embarrassment isn't only due to my resentment at playing the part of the prodigal son: I am also uncertain as to how my father will react. Will he give me back the flat? Or will he, seeing as he's hardly a generous type, refuse? I watch his benign, inscrutable face with ill-concealed anxiety. Then I see him smile as he replies: "It goes without saying that I never took your giving up the inheritance seriously. So all I did was administer the property on your behalf. In other words, the flat is yours."

I am now struck by the fact that my father, in his own words, never took me seriously. Shouldn't I hit back violently at this affectionate demonstration of contempt? Before realizing what I'm saying, I'm overcome by a sense of gratitude as spontaneous as it is unexpected: "Dad, Silvia and I will be eternally grateful for your understanding, your generosity."

73

My father interrupts: "Slowly does it. The flat's yours, but you can't move in right away. It's still being rented as a solicitor's office. You're in luck though, because the solicitor died recently and the office is moving. But it'll all take a while, if only to make the place liveable again."

Moved, my eyes watering with humiliating tears, I say: "Thanks, Dad."

How many years is it since I last said "Dad"? More than twenty perhaps, if I ever said it at all. Launched now on the slippery slope of filial gratitude, I lay it on all the thicker: "It's a big flat, isn't it? How many rooms?"

Strangely, right as I'm coming out with these words, a memory floats to the surface of my mind. It's the memory of an old film from the Thirties that I saw a while back in a cineclub in Paris: *The Traitor*, by John Ford. I remember in particular a scene in the film where, during the struggle against the English, an Irish drunk informs on an IRA member and then goes to the English headquarters to collect the pay-off for his betrayal. The commander has somebody bring a wad of notes and, with a gesture of contempt, as though not wanting to dirty his hands, pushes them across the table with a riding-whip in the direction of the informer. I'm perfectly aware that this memory isn't appropriate: my father isn't an oppressor and I'm not a traitor; but at the same time I do realize that the memory comes out of an acute sense of having suffered a humiliating and final defeat. Meanwhile, my father, annoyed perhaps by my gratitude, answers vaguely: "I don't know, six or eight rooms. It's certainly big, it takes up a whole floor."

With what is by now conscious masochism, I insist: "And can one go and see it? No special reason, but I think Silvia would like to see it."

"Of course, you can see it when you like. Just get the porter to give you the keys."

Suddenly I think I understand why I hate my father. Because I sense he's stronger than I am. Yet at the same time I don't know why he's stronger. Probably if I knew that, I'd stop hating him.

I'm still in the midst of these angry reflections when the door is pushed brusquely open and in comes Fausta carrying a tray with the wherewithal for the injection. With an air of complicity towards me that only increases my embarrassment, she announces: "I'm ready, Professor. Do you want Mr Edoardo to go out?"

Fed up, I look at my father. And then, to my and certainly to Fausta's surprise, he says calmly: "No, why? There's no need for Edoardo to go out. Let's get on with it."

Thus, for reasons that escape me, my father doesn't want to be on his own with Fausta this time. So Fausta was lying perhaps this morning, slandering him? Or was she? I didn't get the impression she was lying when she complained about his persistent Don Juan-style advances, which are typical anyway of certain kinds of invalids. Inspired by Fausta's accusation, I'd been imagining the injection scene with some amusement: Fausta leaning over him, syringe in hand; him pulling down his trousers and at the same time maybe half-moving to stroke those pert breasts; Fausta quite simply pushing his hand away and ordering him to turn over ... A patient's life is made up of these small details, whether he be a miserable nonentity or a famous university professor.

I had looked forward to the scene with malevolent confidence. And instead here was my father by some mysterious instinct avoiding the trap. In the meantime Fausta comes up to the bed and, holding the syringe in the air with one hand, pulls away the bedclothes with a single tug of the other to reveal my father's body stretched out motionless on the undersheet. Too motionless, I can't help thinking, because he should at least help Fausta undo his pyjama-trousers and push them down to his knees. Instead, inexplicably, he stays put, arms slack along his sides, while Fausta, still using just one hand, undoes his pyjama-cord and yanks down the trousers a bit at a time. At this point he should finally roll over and present his buttocks. But he doesn't. For a moment that to me seems interminable, he stays quite still, naked from the waist to the knees, his penis, as usual, in a state of semi-erection, nestling in full view in the tangle of pubic hair over the bag of his big testicles. Needless to say, I can't believe my eyes – Fausta standing there with the syringe ready in her hand and my father looking at his penis with an authoritarian, self-satisfied expression, as if to have her realize that he is quite exceptionally well-hung and that she must appreciate this and take account of it in her dealings with him. But is this exhibition really aimed at Fausta? The doubt crosses my mind when my father stops staring at his crotch and raises his eyes in my direction. The look I surprise in his deep flashing eyes definitely seems to express an ill-concealed thrill of challenge. Yes, no doubt about it, my father wants me to notice and marvel at his virility in a silent contest in which Fausta is called upon to act as judge and referee.

Perhaps Fausta is also aware of my father's exhibitionism, because in a tone of indulgent impatience, she suddenly says: "Come on, roll over now," an ambiguous remark where the word "now" serves to indicate the excessive duration of the exhibition. My father obeys, though not entirely. True, he does turn over, does let her push the needle into a buttock, waits while the liquid is injected, and then rolls on his back again. But while he does all this, he bounces his genitals up and down with a suspicious nonchalance too indecent to be unconscious. Finally, he's sitting up again with his back against the pillows and the bedclothes pulled over his stomach. He seems a little upset and confused. He turns to me sharply and says: "While we're about it, can you please tell me why you've been going on about this nuclear business so much lately?"

While we're about what? I can find no other explanation for his question than that it's a clumsy attempt to have me forget the sexual challenge he's just thrown at me. With an effort I get out: "I go on about it because there is something diabolical in splitting the atom, and the devil, as we all know, is not someone you can ignore."

My father seems almost grateful to be given this opportunity to engage in a discussion he usually tries to avoid. "Diabolical!" he retorts. "Why? It's a useful discovery so long as it's used for peaceful purposes."

"Think about it for a moment: to extract the energy of millions of tonnes of gelignite from a few kilos of uranium! It's diabolical because it has all the appearances of being a miracle."

"So, if it's a miracle, you should call it divine, not diabolical."

Without smiling I reply: "God made the world, that's His miracle. Miracles in the sense of supernatural interventions are usually the work of the devil."

Good-humouredly, my father exclaims: "So, long live the devil!"

I go on seriously: "Let's forget the devil. Let's say that your analysts could have foreseen certain truly diabolical results of their analyses, of their curiosity that is, and done something about it while there was still time."

Oddly enough my father shifts from good humour to irritation: "Why on earth should they? It's up to the generals and politicians to do something about it. What have the scientists got to do with it?" He's silent a moment, then adds in an informative, didactic voice: "You know as well as I do that there are no historical precedents for scientists spontaneously disinventing their own inventions."

I hunt for a metaphor and finally say with more flair than conviction: "Ulysses had himself tied to the mast of his ship and his ears stopped with wax so as not to hear the sirens singing."

This time my father simply bursts out in friendly laughter: "Not bad, scientific research likened to a nice young girl, half-woman half-fish, not bad at all!"

I realize it's time I went. My father is too exhilarated by the conviction that he's got a bigger tool between his legs than I have. To beat him in the argument I'd have to pull down my pants and show him my own claim to virility. Better get out quick. I stand up brusquely: "Well, Dad, I'm off, and thanks again for the flat."

As I close the door he shouts after me: "Don't thank me. Just tell Silvia not to be mad at me any more. The place of her own is ready and waiting."

CHAPTER FIVE

Love in the Chinese Restaurant

∽∾

I'm in the Chinese restaurant again, in a booth this time, sitting on a bench with my back to the wooden partition. Since I generally come early so as to be able to talk in peace with Silvia, the restaurant is deserted. Behind the wall of the booth I can hear rustling, footsteps and whispers that seem to come from the kitchen. While waiting for Silvia, I wonder how I should go about telling her that I've been to ask my father for help and that he immediately promised to give me back the flat. I am still convinced that Silvia left because she was disappointed about not having a place of her own, but at the same time, I am perfectly well aware that our future relationship will depend on the way I announce the unhoped-for solution to the problem that torments and divides us. Mentally, I go over what I should and should not do. One, I must not present the agreement with my father as a victory, but as a tactical retreat. Two, I must stress that I still think of my father as a representative figure of the society I have always rebelled against. Three, I must minimize the advantages of the agreement, say that it's only a temporary solution. Four, I must insist that we find a rented place as soon as possible and that I will then give up my mother's flat once again. As you can see, what worries me most of all is the image of valiant rebel that I would like Silvia to have of me. The curious side to this vanity of mine in my relationship with my wife is that I know perfectly well that Silvia really couldn't care less whether I was or still am a rebel. The truth is, I'm worried about what Silvia will think of me as about what I'll think she thinks.

But here comes Silvia. As on previous occasions, she's wearing her leather jacket, her long, thin, Modigliani neck rising out of it with wistful delicacy. She hasn't got a skirt on today though. Instead she's wearing a pair of bright red trousers, so tight they seem to be separating the lips of her sex between her legs with a neat, fine cut from which a score of straight creases radiate fan-wise like rays of a rising sun. I'm once again struck by Silvia's dual nature, the spirituality of her facial expression and then the sensuality of this certainly not unplanned exhibitionism. My gaze doesn't escape her. Squeezing with some difficulty between bench and table into the booth, she asks: "What are you looking at?"

"Your trousers. They're so tight. Don't they bother you?"

Good-humoured and provocative, she answers: "Not me, what about you?"

Quite suddenly, all my preparation, my calculations vis-à-vis the announcement of the agreement with my father, all go up in smoke. I reach out a hand to take hers and say emotionally: "You realize that I want you?"

"I know," she replies calmly, "I saw it in your eyes.'

"I want you and can't have you."

She looks at me with an almost bureaucratic air of understanding, the way a polite shop assistant behind her counter will listen to the complaints of a customer. "I've already told you any number of times: come to my aunt's when she's not there. If you don't want to, that's your problem."

I ask: "But don't you think there's a contradiction between the fact that you don't want to live with me and this invitation to come and make love at your aunt's place?"

She answers serenely: "I don't see any contradiction. They are two different things that haven't got anything to do with each other."

I realize that going on with the argument won't get me anywhere and so, almost in spite of myself, I announce the arrangement with my father: "It doesn't matter, I'll wait. In fact, while we're on the subject, I think the flat problem really is about to sort itself out."

"How?"

Silvia's tone of voice isn't encouraging, as if, deep down, she wanted to prolong our present pro tem relationship. In fact she adds: "You still think I left because of the flat. But I didn't. Even if you were to find a place tomorrow, I might decide to go on living on my own."

I try not to give much importance to her objection and push on: "Of course, you're free not to accept. But if you don't accept, you'll have to tell me why. If your reasons are sensible, I promise to respect them."

I think I've said everything. Everything, of course, bar the arrangement with my father, an arrangement I'm ashamed of and that even now I'd be glad not to have made. Silvia seems to sense my reticence because she remarks under her breath: "What a lot of introduction. I hope it's not a hole of a place with two rooms and a kitchen."

"On the contrary, it's a very big flat."

"So where is it?"

I realize that now, like it or not, I'll have to tackle the news of the agreement. Sure in the knowledge that Silvia isn't capable of understanding me, and that therefore it's not worth wasting time explaining, I reply: "The flat is on the third floor of our block. It was my part of my mother's estate. I had in fact refused the inheritance and passed it on to my father. I didn't need it and I didn't want to own property. But now that we're married everything has changed, so I decided to ask him to give it back to me."

Incredulous and vehement, Silvia bursts out: "You talked to your father about it?"

God knows why, but this unexpected reaction of hers provokes a similar reaction in me. In a different voice, I say: "Yes, I did, there was nothing else I could do. What would you rather I did? Rob a bank?"

She answers in exactly the way I don't want her to: "I think that given your political convictions you shouldn't have gone to your father."

I'm furious: "Why not? He may see things differently from me, but he's still my father."

"Ever since we met you've done nothing but run him down. And now you go and ask him to help you."

I explode: "And you of all people have the gall to come and tell me I'm a coward! It was you who forced me to go and play prodigal son, running off like that. You knew all along that my political beliefs made it impossible for me to go to my father without surrendering my self-respect! And now you come and criticize me for trying to satisfy your filthy goddammed sick craving to have a filthy goddammed roof owned exclusively by yourself over your head!"

I'm not shouting, but my low, angry voice has the intensity of a shout.

Silvia looks at me bewildered, then says in a desperate voice: "You know what I think? I think it'd be better if we stopped seeing each other."

My heart sinks. "But why?" I exclaim. "What's got into you now?"

My distress doesn't escape her. In a low voice she asks: "So you think it's sick to want to have a home?"

She is thus implicitly admitting that she did, as I've always thought, leave because of the flat problem. Still beside myself with anger, I retort: "No, but it is sick to let the problem destroy your relationship with your husband."

Perhaps she's had a moment to reflect and understand me, because in a contrite, reasonable voice she says: "I'm sorry, don't bother about me, go on. So you went to your father, and . . ."

My voice is calmer too as I finish her sentence: "And spoke to him about our difficulties."

"And your father?"

I want to tell the whole truth now, not hide anything any more: "He said he'd never taken my decision to give up the inheritance seriously, just as, though this is my own personal impression, he never took any of the protest movement seriously. He simply looked after the flat for me and now he's giving it back to me. So, we can go and live there, right away if we want."

I think for a moment, then conclude with jarring irony: "In short, the prodigal son has come home and his father has slain the fatted calf."

Silvia says nothing, so I pick up again, trying to explain my father's behaviour this time: "Apart from the prodigal-son side, though, I did find him incredibly agreeable. Not that he's mean, but he's always been rather attached to things. I think he was ready to come to an agreement with me partly out of a delayed sense of guilt. He ought to have offered us the flat when we got married. Your running away must have made him feel ashamed of himself."

Silvia shakes her head: "Wouldn't it be simpler to put his behaviour down to affection?"

I shake my head: "I don't think my father really has any affection for me. If anything, the opposite. The other day, for example, I surprised him acting in – how can I put it? – making a gesture of sexual rivalry that wasn't exactly affectionate."

"Sexual rivalry? What are you on about?"

In a would-be superficial, conversational voice, I tell her the story of how he showed off his penis during the injection ceremony. I would like it to sound like an amused observation of idiosyncratic behaviour, nothing more. But Silvia listens seriously, without a smile. In the end, she says: "Perhaps he was just being careless and you mistook it for exhibitionism."

"One may be mistaken over ideas, but not with feelings and my feeling was that I was being confronted by an old man who was showing me his tool as if to say: 'mine's bigger than yours'."

Silvia says nothing. She watches me with listless, motionless eyes. Finally she seems to make up her mind: "You talk about the flat in your block as if it was already decided I was going to live there. But that's not how things stand. The fact that you've found a flat doesn't mean that I'm coming back to live with you. Seeing as you can't or won't understand this, we'd better have it out once and for all."

I haven't followed any of this, but a sudden shiver runs down my spine and I feel thoroughly shaken: "What do you mean?"

She replies hurriedly: "I haven't got anything against living in this flat in theory, but you don't seem to want to understand that there's another reason why I'm not sure whether I'll accept your offer or not. The fact is I've got another man."

I'm already so worked up that this revelation arouses more amazement than anything else. Why on earth didn't I think of it before? Then, together with an aching sense of loss, I feel ashamed of my chatter about the flat and the story of my father's supposed exhibitionism. "But why didn't you tell me right away? Why did you let me go on and on about my father and his stupid flat?"

"I tried to make you see, but it was as if you were blind, and then maybe I was ashamed of admitting it."

"What's there to be ashamed about, admitting you love another man?"

Lowering her head, she says: "The fact is, I don't love this man." Then I realize to my surprise that this, for me, flattering response doesn't actually give me any relief at all. No, because this declaration of Silvia's has settled one question, why she left me, only to open another: if she doesn't love him, then why is this man so important as to have her leave the husband she does love? All at once I feel overwhelmed by a sick feeling of tiredness. I say coldly: "I don't want to hear any more, but since that's how things stand, it seems pointless for us to go on seeing each other."

Silvia doesn't speak. She stares at me from wide eyes, but seems not to see me. Then comes the explanation for this staring, dreamy gaze of hers: to my surprise, because I didn't expect it from someone so rational and unemotional as Silvia usually is, two very small, pinched tears run down from her eyes to stop and then lose themselves almost immediately in the upper part of her cheeks. It's a mysterious kind of crying, simply because there are so few tears, and I suddenly feel the same mixture of doubt and incredulity as the believer who, kneeling in the gloom of a church, thinks he has seen the statue of a madonna renowned for her miracles crying in the same uncertain way. Is Silvia crying, or is it a hallucination? To make sure, I ask her, "But why are you crying? What's wrong?" almost afraid that she'll tell me she isn't crying at all.

Instead she acknowledges her tears with an oddly resentful tone: "I'm crying because I'd like to go on seeing you."

"But if you've got another man?"

"If I go on seeing you, perhaps I'll finally make up my mind."

"Make up your mind about what?"

"To leave him."

"A few moments ago," I say, as though thinking aloud, "it was you who didn't want us to see each other any more. Now it's me. What should we do?"

"Go on seeing each other."

"And then?"

"Then, I don't know."

"What don't you know?"

"I don't know what will happen. I've got a crush on this man, perhaps it'll go away."

I sense that the word "crush", a frivolous, juvenile expression for falling in love, is at once appropriate and inadequate. Appropriate because it indicates the short-lived nature of Silvia's infatuation; inadequate because it doesn't express its irresistible violence. "It seems to me," I hazard, "that 'crush' isn't the right word."

"So what would you call it?"

"I don't know. Passion."

"No, Dodo," she explains calmly, "it really is a crush, the kind you get at eighteen. The kind that when it's over you ask yourself: but how could I have gone and lost my head for a man like that?"

Cautiously, I suggest: "Crushes don't last very long. Whereas this . . ."

I'm hoping she'll tell me how long her betrayal has been going on. But she doesn't fall into the trap, just agrees vaguely: "Perhaps this won't last long either. But for the moment I've got it and I can't do anything about it."

"What do you mean you can't do anything? All you have to do is decide not to see him any more."

"Right, but that's exactly what I find it impossible to do. I've done my best to stop seeing him, really my very best. But then I run into him and . . ."

"And what?"

"And I'm back where I started. I can't help it."

"There's nothing we can't help. There mustn't be."

"Yes, I thought the same myself. But you know what happens? That exactly because you don't want to do certain things, you maybe find yourself enjoying them even more."

"Enjoying them more how?"

"It's as if you wanted to put out a fire only you make a mistake and instead of water you throw petrol over it. Perhaps I wouldn't go back to him if I didn't take it all so seriously, if I didn't swear to myself never to go back to him again."

She speaks with growing abandon and fluency and I'm struck by the humiliating suspicion that I'm serving as confidant to my wife in her adulterous relationship with an unknown lover. But the desire to know more, to know everything, gets the better of me and in the end, to quote Silvia's own words, I can't help myself.

I say: "But can't you at least tell me why this man you don't love turns out to be so irresistible?"

She shakes her head: "Look, I'd rather not talk about it. And then I wouldn't have mentioned it if you hadn't forced me to by going on about the flat thing. I only told you because you were so far from the truth and I felt bad about leading you on."

"No, I don't care, I want you to tell me everything. Who is he? What does he do? What's he like? Everything."

"But why?"

Exasperated, I shout: "But don't you understand that I'll only really be able to believe you love me and not him if you tell me everything about him?"

"And if I don't tell you everything?"

"Don't you remember what you said not long before we got married?"

"What?"

"You're the man of my life," you said.

"It was true. It's still true."

"Yes, but if you don't tell me everything, I'll think he's the man of your life now."

"It's not true, nothing's really changed between us."

"So what is he? The man you're betraying the man of your life with?"

With disconcerting reasonableness she accepts this: "It's a funny way of putting it, but probably that's the truth."

I'm furious: "And you tell me just like that?"

"How am I supposed to tell you?"

This time I say nothing, my head down. Silvia starts talking again in that intimate, confidential tone, which, like I said, humiliates me and automatically makes me what I don't, in any circumstances, want to be: the understanding friend a woman can confide in without embarrassment. "Everything, really everything, I can't tell you. There are some things you can't say, not just because one's ashamed of them, but because if you say them just like that, on their own, in isolation, they give an incomplete, false idea of what's going on."

Brusquely and angrily, I say: "I don't understand what the hell you're on about."

She looks at me and obviously realizes I'm suffering because her face assumes that expression of sorrow and pity typical of Silvia in her best moments. She protests: "But Dodo, why do you want to know all these things about the intimate side of life? It's difficult for me to tell you these things and it won't make you happy to hear them. So?"

"But what things?"

She looks at me a while, then in a condescending voice, like a schoolmistress with a particularly childish pupil, begins: "You asked for it, mind! Now let's imagine that someone were to ask me what happens between us at certain moments. What do you think this inquisitive person would think about the way you make love?"

"I don't know," I reply, a shade unsettled, "what's so special about the way we make love?"

"Not we. You," she corrects. "Nothing special at all until you get down to the details."

"But what are you talking about?"

"I think our inquisitive friend would think that you make love with your eyes."

Suddenly remembering Pascasie and her light-hearted insinuation that I was a voyeur, I exclaim: "Now you're accusing me of being a Peeping Tom."

Smiling, she says: "There, you see. You get worked up if I tell you you're a voyeur, and you're right to be worked up because there's more between us than just the fact that you watch me. And the same thing's true of my relationship with this man I've got the crush on. To say certain things would give a false and incomplete idea of the relationship."

At this point I want to hear more about my own way of

making love; partly because I sense that through talking about this I'll get to know about "their" way. To encourage her, I remark: "You're the second person who's told me I'm a voyeur lately."

"Who's the other."

"A friend. A woman."

She shows no interest in knowing who this woman is. "You see," she cries, "I'm not the only person who says so."

"Okay, but what is my way of making love, then?"

She eyes me for a moment, then explains: "You always make love the same way. You lie on your back and want me to climb on top. You see, just describing the way we make love, I've already given a false, incomplete, crude idea of it. But let's go on. Why do you want me to be on top and you below? I often used to wonder and then you told me yourself: so as to watch me better, in a more detached, more contemplative way. And in fact you sometimes tell me that while we're making love my face reminds you of the face of a madonna in a church your mother took you to when you were a boy. So what is all this, if not a kind of, maybe, mystic voyeurism? That's certainly the feeling I get; so much so that this sort of religious idea you have of me has quite an influence on the way I act when we make love. I sense that you *want* me to look like a madonna so I try not to show the pleasure I'm feeling and make an effort to keep my face serene, immobile and impassive, even though, if I let myself go, God knows what faces I might pull, the kind people do of course when they're making love! What an effort, though, pretending to be a madonna when the man you love is fucking you."

I'm not used to hearing Silvia use bad language and I start. She notices and adds: "I'm sorry, but it's the truth."

I protest: "So people who go to church and lift their eyes

to the holy image while they're kneeling are voyeurs then?"

"In a certain sense, yes."

"But the voyeur spies on people. I don't spy on you when we're making love, like a voyeur would, to see if your face contorts in spasms of pleasure. On the contrary, I like to see you impassive, serene, without grimaces or spasms."

She shakes her head: "Maybe so. But madonna apart, my impression is that when you make love you do more looking than anything else." She thinks, then reaches out an affectionate hand and takes mine: "Dodo, when it comes to love, one needn't be ashamed of anything. You love through your eyes. That's all. And then sometimes I've enjoyed this eye-love and didn't disguise the fact. Even if you weren't looking at me in quite the way the faithful look at the madonna."

"But when?" I ask, faintly stirred.

She smiles: "Have you forgotten already? In Forte dei Marmi, before we knew each other, when you flirted with me from the window of your *pension*."

I haven't forgotten at all. On the contrary, I remember very well. I was staying in a *pension* in the pinewood by the sea. It was very near another one and I could see a wall with a few windows, all closed except for the one exactly opposite mine. One afternoon, I'd gone to my room for a nap and was already closing the shutters when I noticed that the window opposite was wide open, giving me a complete view of the room. It was a room like any other, the sort they usually have in these small seaside hotels, but perhaps precisely because it was so common, I found it mysterious; it had that obscurely significant mystery that insignificant things do have. Most of all I remember the colours, every single one of them; they seemed gay and fresh, perhaps because I was looking at them so hungrily, as if to feed my famished vision. In the middle was the bed, painted green with a yellow coverlet. In one corner there was a red cupboard. The floor was tiled blue. At the foot of the bed was an ochre-coloured armchair. The seats and backs of the chairs were orange. The walls were whitewashed. What else? Oh yes, a big Florentine straw hat, pale yellow with a black ribbon, hung from a coat hook; a pair of pink sandles with red heels were poking out from under the bed; a green-and-blue striped dressing gown had been thrown across the armchair. Finally, the bathroom door was a glaring ultramarine blue.

I had the impression of a scene at the theatre. The curtain had risen, but the actors, or rather the actress (because there could be no doubt that the occupant of the room was a woman) hadn't made her entry yet. So instead of closing the shutters, I just pulled them to and started to wait, standing there with my eye to the crack and with that somehow cruel patience of the hunter lying in wait for his prey. She had to come back to her room some time and I would wait just as long as it took, until evening if necessary, until the following day. It was very hot; you could hear the June bugs droning in the pine branches. Although aware that my watching amounted to snooping, I felt a happy sense of well-being, as if I were doing something I had a natural talent for. So much so that after a while I felt there was no need to hide any more and I opened the shutters wide. I didn't just want to see now, but to be seen as well, to be noticed while I watched.

Finally, after a wait of almost half an hour, the bedroom door opened and Silvia came in. Since the door was exactly opposite my window, she could hardly help but look back at me. Her face took on a half-surprised, half-puzzled expression and I imagined, logically enough, that her first move would be to close the shutters. With the result that I felt in advance a sense of frustration and guilt; she would shut the window in my face now, and automatically, I would become just the usual indiscreet and out-of-luck voyeur.

But it didn't turn out like that. Silvia moved across the room, threw me another glance, obviously aware I was there, then disappeared into the bathroom. She came out a few moments later and once again, with a by-now undisguised complicity, didn't go to close the shutters. All at once I was sure that she was responding to my voyeurism with a corresponding exhibitionism and my heart began to beat faster.

Silvia moved to and fro about the room, doing the most insignificant things with the concentration of the actress who senses she is being watched by a large and attentive audience. She moved to and fro and with every step her flowing yellow skirt flapped around her legs as if in a provocative dance. Finally, she stood in the middle of the room and with a brusque gesture, like a marionette, bent down, legs apart, took hold of the hem of her skirt and pulled it up and off over her head. From then on the game between us grew faster and faster, more and more arousing. And yet I wasn't feeling the kind of excitement people imagine a voyeur out for smut must feel. The truth is I had managed to create, almost immediately, a chaste, natural relationship between Silvia and myself, between my observation and her apparition. It was a relationship where love with its questions and answers, its surrender and trust, was already present.

So the show went on. Having taken off her skirt, Silvia threw it on the armchair, then went to the mirror over the dresser and, standing so as to show me her profile, slipped off her bra and curved her hands in two cups under her breasts, weighing them and pushing them up a little as if to study their shape and volume. Then she let them fall again and touched the nipples with her fingers in a delicate, contemplative way, as though checking their sensitivity. In short, by now she was no longer pretending to ignore me with an innocent naturalness; she was playing stripper with the obvious intention of producing certain effects rather than others. In fact every now and then she would throw me a quick sidelong glance as though to make sure I was still there and not unhappy with the performance.

The contemplation of her bust didn't end when she dropped two hands to her waist to roll down her pants. Dazed and thoughtful she went on looking at her breasts while distractedly exposing her crotch, as if she had something on her mind which only had to do with the upper half of her body. Almost immediately I understood what she was up to: she wanted to show me the thick, dark pubic hair that thrust out aggressively under the curve of her rump, and she wanted to show it in profile, because only in profile would I be able to see its curious bristling quality, like the hackles of a frightened cat. Not satisfied with that, she ran a hand through the hairs to fluff them up and have them bristle out after their long constriction under her pants. At this point the performance, so like a normal striptease, yet different because of our unexpected, mutual feeling of love, seemed to be over. Silvia pulled a chair into the middle of the room, picked up a guitar propped against the wall, and, bending her head over the instrument, began to strum some chords. The position reminded me of the viola-playing angels you sometimes see in old paintings; except that the angels keep one leg crossed over the other, while at the centre of Silvia's groin, in the brown bush of her hair, I could see the white of a cotton-wool tampon. Did Silvia know that apart from her naked body she was also showing me something men usually find repugnant? Of course she knew. But showing me the tampon must have been, for her, like an unconscious challenge to my incipient love. Because only love is capable of transforming repugnance into attraction.

But the exhibitionism aroused by my voyeurism had by now exhausted its invention. Silvia played the guitar for a while, then, as if suddenly bored, got up and, without hurrying, came to the window and closed the shutters.

The next day I looked for her on the beach, found her and had myself introduced by a friend we had in common. Thus, from the encounter of a casual exhibitionism with an unplanned voyeurism, was born a very normal love relationship, which, a year later, was to lead to our marriage.

At the end of this lightning recollection, I say: "I know, our love began with looking. But why were you so happy for me to look at you then, and so bothered by it now?"

"I don't know," she answers vaguely. "It was summer, it was very hot and I felt dazed by the heat. When I saw you watching me from your window, I thought: if it makes him happy, it doesn't cost me anything, why not?"

"Is that all? Didn't you feel anything yourself?"

"Yes, I did feel something perhaps. I liked you, Dodo. You didn't look like a voyeur at all, more like somebody at the theatre, watching the performance in a detached way. But you know what?"

"What?"

"After closing the shutters I lay down on the bed and masturbated."

"You never told me that!"

"You never asked."

She is quiet for a moment. "The next day, when you got yourself introduced, I had a strange sensation."

"What?"

95

"I said to myself in amazement: I feel like I've already made love with this man."

I feel reassured by this. I say gently: "Now that you've described my way of making love, tell me how you do it with him."

This time, I don't know whether out of tiredness or trust, she doesn't hold back, doesn't hesitate; with brutal frankness she says: "I know this will disappoint you, seeing as when we make love you always look at me as if I were the madonna, but I'm not the madonna."

She falls silent a moment, then goes on, staring right into my eyes: "I'm a pig, and I like to make love like a pig."

With an effort I ask: "How do pigs make love?"

"The animal way. I read it in an old guide for saying confession: *more ferarum*."

"But which animals?"

"Dogs, horses: it was the first time I'd done it that way. It was a revelation."

"But why?"

"I don't know. Perhaps because I turn my back to him and he can't see me, so that I can pull all the faces I want; perhaps because, unlike you, he's the active one and I'm passive; perhaps because . . ."

At this point Silvia breaks off and bows her head.

"Perhaps because what?" I insist.

She raises her head again to show me a smiling face: "Oh God, Dodo, why do you want to know everything, absolutely everything?"

"You know why," I reply angrily. "Because even if only in words I want you to betray him with me."

She doesn't seem to notice what I've said. After glancing round the restaurant, she says under her breath: "Okay, listen: right at the moment of climax, he says: 'Tell me you're my pig.' And I have to repeat: 'Yes, I'm your pig.' "

"Have to? You don't have to do anything. You like saying it and you say it, and that's that."

"No, I have to."

"But why?"

"Because he's on top of me; he forces my head down on the table and whispers in my ear: 'If you don't say it, I'll break your neck.' "

"Brutal, huh?"

"Some things seem brutal when you describe them straight off like this. But the voice that says those words isn't brutal."

"So what is it?"

"It's the voice of love."

"But do you love him?"

"I've already told you, I don't love him."

This time I fall silent. The roof has fallen in on my world and I'm in a state of near delirium searching through the ruins.

Silvia seems aware of my distress, because she reaches out a hand and says: "Come on, don't be so sad. After all, it's better to be treated like a madonna than a cow. I'm going through an animal phase, then I'll get back to being your sacred image, okay?"

She squeezes my fingers, a little excitedly, as if to rouse me into saying or doing something. Suddenly I say: "Let's make love, here, now."

"What?"

"Let's do it the way we did it the first time, by looking."

"By looking? What do you mean?"

"Let me see you."

This time Silvia understands and turns to glance round the restaurant. "Here? But how?"

"We are out of the way in this booth, no one can see us. You come and sit next to me, between me and the wall.

97

You open your pants, just for a moment, and I'll look at you."

Taking pity, she asks: "You love me that much?"

I nod, unable to speak. Silvia looks round, then gets up, goes round the table and comes back in the booth on my side. I shift to the outside of the bench and she sits between me and the wall. Then she lies back, takes hold of her zip and pulls it right down with a single tug. Her hands go to widen the opening above pale-blue panties plump with a dark shadow. She pushes them down and arches back on the seat, her rump thrust upward. Out of her trousers, that strange pubic fleece of hers rears up like an aggressive crest, all the hairs standing on end as if in a fury. She says gently: "You can touch me if you want. But just for a moment."

"No, I only need to look."

She looks down at herself too and says: "Isn't it better the way other women have it? Flat and soft as velvet?"

"No, I like it like this, like a brush."

She says: "I'm going to touch myself now. Tell me something else it makes you think of."

I see her sink her hand between her legs: "It makes me think of the hackles of a frightened cat."

"And then?"

"Of a cock's crest."

"And then, quick, something else."

"The plume of a helmet."

"And another?"

"A Phrygian cap."

"Something else."

"The sun rising with all its rays."

"Yes, the sun's rays, yes."

Silvia sighs, stretches out some more and sighs again, lifting her stomach while her pubic hair thrusts stiffly

upward. Finally she falls back, eyes closed, as if exhausted.
I reach down and pull up her zip. Silvia opens her eyes.
"Thanks," I tell her.

Silvia shakes her head as though still unable to speak.
Then she manages to get out: "Thanks for what?"

"For doing what you did."

She gets up now and slips by me out of the booth, saying:
"I've really got to be going."

"Do me a last favour."

"What?"

"Seeing as I've made love to you with my eyes, now
close them."

"But how?"

"Pass a hand over them."

"But that's what you do to a corpse."

"Right."

She reaches out a hand and passes the palm quickly
over my eyes. I lower my eyelids. When I open them again
she has already disappeared leaving only the tinkling of
the carillon.

Chapter Six

The Devil who Watches

❧

Today, unusually, I don't go for my regular early afternoon walk. I don't even think of going. After eating with my father, I hang around in the house reading a book I'm not interested in. But then, towards five, seized by a sudden inspiration, I leave the flat in a rush and set off in the car in the direction of the part of the Tiber where Pascasie lives. I'm not really sure why I'm going there and this uncertainty fills me with a sense of distrust towards myself, as though towards someone I don't really know very well and who could, I suspect, have some surprises in store for me as a result.

Will I go and see Pascasie again? Perhaps, but I'm not entirely sure. If I do go and see her it will be to check out an impression I had during the first visit: the impression that Pascasie, like Mallarmé's black woman, is possessed by a demon; not the demon of lechery though, as in the poem, but, more subtly, the demon of a kind of hostile desire to draw me into temptation. What gave me this impression was the cold, calculating, watchful way she never stopped spying on me throughout my visit.

I know why she was watching me of course: to see if I would give in to the temptation, the literary nature of which eluded her, to ask her to act out the scene described by Mallarmé in his poem. It goes without saying that Pascasie had no intention of satisfying such a request, just as I had no intention of making it.

What she wanted was to see me slip on the temptation, as though on your common-or-garden banana-skin, with, in the end, the same comic and reductive effects. As I had told her, there was a cynical exhibitionist in her who, the precise moment she exhibited herself, turned into a mischievous voyeur.

But why did Pascasie want to lead me into temptation? It occurs to me that the explanation can be found without leaving Mallarmé's poem; it's there in the first line: "A negress possessed by the devil". The fact is that the person watching me wasn't Pascasie, but the devil who apparently possesses her. A voyeuristic devil who wanted to lead me into temptation quite simply so as to enjoy the spectacle of the effects of his victory over me. Yes, a voyeur-devil who wanted to contemplate a world made in his own image and likeness. So, if I do go and see Pascasie today, it will be to exorcize the devil, to reclaim the innocent, cheerful African woman I spoke to from the pavement during my early afternoon walk.

The sky is uniformly covered today by a low, dark, stormy cloud mass: no shifting cumulus, no rents of blue. With the result, I tell myself, that I can't even offer my usual obsessive fantasizing of an atomic mushroom rising from behind the dome of St Peter's as a pretext for this incursion into Pascasie's territory. It's clear that I'm going to Pascasie's place and nowhere else; but it's equally clear that I don't know why I'm going there.

I arrive at the Tiber and the red-and-white barrier blocking the road. I park the car, get out, lock the door and only then turn to take a look at the dome of St Peter's. In the dull, still air the dome has a washed out, dirty-brown colour, not at all imposing, lost rather among the inglorious modern housing projects that seem to close in on it more tightly than usual today. I look at it and am amazed that on other occasions I saw it as a symbol of the world the atomic bomb will destroy, in the next few years perhaps. Yes, I think, the war, if it comes, will certainly destroy it. But why talk of symbols? The very fact that the bomb has been invented has destroyed the world spiritually long before destroying it materially. The bomb is only the final flowering of something which began a long time ago, just as the dome was the final flowering of something else which belongs to a now distant past.

Still looking at the dome as I mull over these thoughts, I'm suddenly almost blinded by a silent streak of lightning that zigzags, forked and vibrant, down through the slate-coloured sky, then is gone. I wait and then, after what seems a very long interval, there is the thunder: it rolls heavily, like an iron ball bouncing across a sheet of metal, and then explodes dry and deafening. Immediately afterwards come the first gusts of a fresh wet wind, promising rain, sending grey whirlwinds of dust and dirt snaking up from the pavement.

But it's not raining yet; the wind drops. Then, right in front of me, I see Pascasie, looking at me and laughing. She's not alone; walking beside her is a young girl, about thirteen maybe. Both Pascasie and the girl are carrying bags of shopping with brown paper parcels and green bunches of vegetables sprouting out. Pascasie is wearing a straight, stiff red coat which goes right down to her very slim ankles. All this red reminds me of the demon, who, according to Mallarmé, goads the negress in the poem. But even without this literary reminder, I'm immediately conscious, as she comes out with a childish laugh, of the presence of some obscure, malevolent scheme lurking in the watchful coldness of her eyes.

Pascasie says: "I've been shopping with Gesuina. I help her and she helps me. Gesuina," she adds, turning to the girl, "this is Mr Dodo, the one I told you about. Shake hands, go on, don't be so shy, he won't eat you. Dodo, Gesuina is the daughter of the woman who looks after our block."

I look at Gesuina. She's tall, narrow-shouldered, thin; she has a pale, sharpish face with big, dull eyes and a small mouth. Her dress is knitted of tobacco-brown wool and perches up on her chest on two immature points. She offers me a big bony hand and, when I shake it, sketches a little curtsy.

Pascasie says: "She'd like to go to school, but her mother wants her to work in the block. So I'm helping her. I'm teaching her French."

Pascasie gives me this information with her usual, muddled, childish cheerfulness. But I'm immediately aware that her eyes are switching from me to Gesuina and back, and that idea of mine that every piece of voyeurism is matched by a corresponding exhibitionism backfires on me, and to my disadvantage. The fact is that Pascasie is watching the way I'm looking at Gesuina. Does she hope, perhaps, that I'll see Mallarmé's little girl in the porter's daughter? Or is it I who am incapable of throwing off the charm of literary analogies? But whatever the truth of the matter, I am certainly being watched and am thus obliged to look away unnaturally towards the barrier at the end of the street.

As though to confirm this idea of mine, Pascasie adds

after a moment: "Pretty, our Gesuina, isn't she?" And she reinforces the praise by curling an arm round the reluctant girl's shoulders and squeezing her.

Awkwardly, I admit: "Yes, she is pretty. How old is she?"

"Fourteen in five months' time," Gesuina replies with a ready innocence that has Pascasie laughing.

"Women always say they're younger than they are and instead you want to be older. Go on with you, let's say you're thirteen and a half, but you look fifteen. So, Dodo, will you walk home with us?"

The three of us set off towards the barrier. Beyond it there is the usual protected, decayed atmosphere. Here and there the tar has swollen and split like a diseased skin: brilliantly green grass grows in the black wounds. Hardly anyone is around: a couple of kids are chasing each other, whirling about on their roller skates; a pair of lovers walk along slowly, arms round each other's waists; a strange character, bald and moustached, sits in a parked car and seems absorbed in solving the crossword puzzle in his paper. The trees are all in bud; the light-green, near-white buds seem out of place against the black backdrop of the sky. It is humid and hot; the air is buzzing and sticky as if full of thousands of invisible midges. I walk with my eyes down, looking at the ground. I am pretty-well certain that Pascasie would like me to take my eyes off the tar and turn them to the girl now walking a few steps ahead of us. In the end Pascasie asks: "Why aren't you saying anything, Dodo? Aren't you going to tell me what you're thinking?"

In a neutral voice, I answer: "I'm thinking about you."

"And what are you thinking about me?"

I take my time, then say slowly: "I was wondering if you'd ever read a novelist called Dostoevsky."

She looks at me suspiciously and says: "No, I haven't."

"Well, Dostoevsky used to fancy little girls like Gesuina. Or so people say, partly because it seems he confessed to another writer that he'd once raped a young girl, and then again because he described a scene like that in his most famous novel."

Pascasie sends me a sidelong glance from distrustful eyes: "What's the novel called?"

"*Crime and Punishment.*"

She cries: "Oh, I've heard of that. Of course: *Crime and Punishment*. Why did you want to know if I'd read it?"

"Because if you had read it, you'd understand that what matters most in a writer is not the things he writes, but how he writes them. Whether he has experienced them or not isn't important. In the poem about the African woman, everything has been invented. In Dostoevsky's book, nothing is invented. The poet has never seen a black woman have sex with a little girl. The novelist, on the other hand, has had sex with a little girl. But the poet's girl is just as real as the novelist's, and vice versa."

Offended, Pascasie exclaims: "What do you want from me, Dodo? I don't understand you."

I answer frankly: "I want you to stop mixing up literature and life. Maybe you're thinking that I go for little girls because I like a poem where a woman has sex with a little girl. But you're wrong. I like the poem, not little girls."

Pascasie gives me a hard look out of the corner of her eye: "Maybe that novelist had sex with a little girl on purpose to find out what it was like so he could write about it later."

"No, on the contrary. He wrote to free himself from what he had done."

Pascasie doesn't give in so soon: "So," she comes back, "he had sex with the girl on purpose to have the remorse so as then to be able to free himself from it by describing it."

I can't help but exclaim: "You know you're intelligent, Pascasie."

She replies a little darkly: "Yes, I know, but you're more intelligent than I am." A somewhat sinister bit of praise, this, which seems to hold an echo of her disappointment at my having so far avoided the traps she keeps laying for me.

We arrive at the garden gate and walk to the door. With the thunderstorm imminent the entrance hall is almost dark. I see Gesuina go to the glass door of the porter's office, open it, look in and call: "Mummy, Mummy!"

From the depths of the semi-basement comes the garbled voice of the mother saying something unintelligible. Gesuina shouts: "I'm going to Pascasie's, Mummy," and at almost the same moment a flash of lightning fills the whole hall with a vivid light. Gesuina is still by the porter's office, but Pascasie is already standing at the open door of her flat, her face turned towards me with an odd expression of cold impatience.

We go in. Like the hall, the flat is dark inside. Pascasie goes ahead of us into the sitting room, exclaiming, almost joyfully: "What horrible weather!" The heavy rain of a cloud-burst is beating against the windows now; it comes in wave after wave, as if thrown in bucketfuls to wash the panes. I see Pascasie put a possessive hand on the girl's neck and push her towards the adjoining kitchen, saying quietly: "Come here a second, there's something I have to tell you."

I'm left alone and sit down on a small Swedish-style chair with the feeling that I'm waiting for something to happen without knowing what. In the meantime I look at the dark, streaming windows and finally tell myself that whatever this something is, I mustn't have anything to do with it, nor let myself get involved in it at any cost.

All of a sudden a bolt of lightning explodes with a tremendous crash very close by – perhaps it went down in the Tiber. Immediately afterwards the rain redoubles its violence and the room grows darker, save for the two windows, which, however, light up nothing but themselves. Then, in the silence that follows the crash of thunder, I distinctly hear two voices, Pascasie's and Gesuina's, talking, or rather arguing, in the kitchen. I can't make out what they're saying at first, but I can distinguish the tones of the voices: Pascasie's insistent and authoritarian; Gesuina's timid, but stubborn. The impression is that Pascasie is giving orders, Gesuina resisting. I'm reminded, logically enough, of Mallarmé's poem, though I think of it as a key to the situation too precise not to be false. The "negress possessed by the devil" and the sad little girl of the poem would certainly have talked in the same way, in the same tones and with the same intensity before coming to their agreement. But there the likeness ends: all the rest is literature. Then, as the patter of rain on the windows eases off, I catch what the two women in the kitchen are talking about. Pascasie, so it seems, is trying to persuade Gesuina to show me her French exercise-book with her homework, and Gesuina is refusing. Then, at last, they appear in the doorway to the sitting room: Pascasie has managed to get her way.

Waving the exercise-book, she says: "She didn't want you to see her homework, she's afraid you'll find some mistakes. But she's really good; look how well she translated this fable."

She hands me the exercise-book and pushes Gesuina towards me. I take the book reluctantly and flick through it. As I do so, I ask: "What fable did you give her to translate?"

"*Perrette au pot au lait*, by La Fontaine."

I say hurriedly: "Excellent translation by the looks of it."

"You see, Gesuina, even the professor says you're good."

I don't know what to do or say. I give the exercise-book back to Gesuina and say to Pascasie: "Why don't you make me a cup of tea?"

I immediately regret this request because Pascasie, with the cruel joy of the hunter at last presented with a visible and unsuspecting prey, exclaims: "A tea! A tea, African-style. I'll see to it right away. You stay here and look at Gesuina's book, and you, Gesuina, listen to what the professor tells you."

I try to stop her. I absolutely don't want to be left alone with the girl: "No, you stay here. Gesuina can get the tea. I'm sure Gesuina knows how to make tea perfectly well, don't you, Gesuina?"

Gesuina makes a little curtsy and asks: "Do you want it strong, or weak?"

Unhappy, Pascasie interrupts: "But you don't know how to make it the African way."

Gesuina's pride is stung: "Yes I do. You taught me yourself."

To cut the argument short, I say firmly: "You go right ahead and make the tea, Gesuina. I'm sure it will be excellent. We'll wait for you here."

And so Gesuina goes out and I'm left alone with Pascasie. Who is not laughing any more. On the contrary, she seems – though always in her very natural, extrovert way – thrown. We watch each other and probably Pascasie sees something like a reproach in my face, because finally she says: "When I was a girl, in my village, my father sent me to the church school, run by an abbot. He was very old. He'd been in Africa for forty years, and he had eyes like a hawk, penetrating eyes that used to search my face as I spoke. When those eyes were watching me I always had the feeling my head had turned to glass and he could see everything I was thinking. Well, you have the same effect on me that that abbot had. I always have the feeling you're reading my mind."

"What makes you say that?"

"Remember the first time you came here? You explained that we were both voyeurs: you were watching me and I was watching you."

"So?"

She starts to laugh: "Oh Dodo, Dodo, it's impossible to hide anything from you. When you told me you wanted tea and I said I'd go and get it and told you to look at Gesuina's exercise-book, you sent me a look as if my head really was made of glass and you were reading what was inside."

"Why?"

"Because you realized I wanted you to be alone with Gesuina."

"Why did you want that?"

She shrugs her shoulders: "Obvious: to see if you fancied her."

"So what would you have done then, if I'd agreed to be alone with Gesuina?"

"Nothing. I would have thought: there, it's really true, he does fancy Gesuina. Just a joke, like any other."

I stay quiet a moment and reflect. I come to the conclusion that she's being sincere, she wasn't intending to go beyond the so-called joke. And yet this joke has an obscure meaning, something hard to pin down: it suggests both hostility towards me, and complicity. Pascasie suddenly grows uneasy at my silence and asks: "Are you offended? Don't worry, I don't think you fancy Gesuina. I just wanted to see if you did."

But here is Gesuina. She comes in slowly, holding a tray with glasses full of steaming-hot tea. In her grating, girlish voice, she says: "I put half the sugar-bowl in it."

Pascasie takes a glass and hands it to me. We drink in silence. The tea is very sweet, thick as a liqueur. Pascasie asks Gesuina: "What about you? Didn't you make some for yourself?"

"It's too sweet for me. Well, I'll be off back to mum now, she's waiting for me." She gets up, makes her little curtsy and goes.

As soon as she's out of the room, Pascasie says: "She was determined not to show you her exercise-book. I had to insist, threaten not to give her any more lessons."

I remark coldly: "Probably she realized the exercise-book was a ploy for leaving her alone with me."

I see her twist her mouth a little in an almost scornful expression. "No, you frightened her as a professor. As a man, you wouldn't have frightened her at all. You've no idea what a flirt she is when she gets the chance."

"Shy with the professor, flirty with the man."

"Right."

I get up and tell her: "Pascasie, I really ought to be off."

Pascasie doesn't try to keep me. She gets up herself and goes ahead of me into the hall. Then she turns and faces me: "If I didn't love John, you'd be the man for me. You're an intellectual and I've always gone for intellectuals."

She reaches out a hand and touches my cheek, staring at me with embarrassing seriousness. She has a long narrow hand with a light, rough, fresh palm. The hand leaves my cheek and slips behind my neck. She pulls me towards her in a strange way, sideways, as if she wanted to say something in my ear, so that I find myself with my ear very close to her mouth. Then, instead of speaking, she kisses my ear, or rather grabs it with her lips, the way you bite at a ripe fruit on a tree. Her mouth opens until it encircles the whole ear and I experience the curious, but not unpleasant sensation that she wants to swallow me up, starting with my outer ear. Then Pascasie steps back and opens the door for me, moving aside to let me go by. Going out, I say: "Bye now, Pascasie," and she replies good-humouredly: "Bye now, my little voyeur."

Out on the road by the river, I can hear my ear ringing as though after a dip in the sea. I lift my hand to my ear: it's still wet with Pascasie's saliva. On the ground, all that remains of the recent downpour are a few black mirrors of puddles reflecting the trees, the breaks of blue sky, the shifting white clouds.

CHAPTER SEVEN

The Book-lined Corridor

It is one o'clock in the morning. I know because I just heard the dull chime of the bell of a small church nearby, a sound more typical of a country village than a big city like Rome. I'm lying on my bed, fully clothed, though without my shoes, reading one of the numerous books on the effects of nuclear war that I've been accumulating for some time in my little library here, a library once made up exclusively of literary texts. Why do I keep reading these books that are all the same and, in the end, boring? Because, as I said at the beginning of this journal, in spite of all my reading and fantasizing, I still can't "think" the atomic bomb, in the sense of mastering the subject in my mind.

Of course in the book it talks about atomic fission and the fact that during the explosion a tiny amount of material is transformed into an enormous quantity of energy. Now this disproportionate transformation never ceases to amaze me; so much so that I talked to a colleague at the university about it, a physics lecturer. He explained that what was really making such an impression on me was the imbalance between mass and energy. But thinking over what he said, I tell myself that it isn't so much the imbalance that amazes me, as something else, which, not having an education in physics, I find it hard to express. To put it briefly, what I can't manage to think is the fact that in certain special conditions created by science, material becomes explosive: that is, that the destruction of this world I find myself living in, is implicit in the composition of the world itself: destruction by fire in a world where, in normal circumstances, fire is rare as a natural, spontaneous state. This world, which in its most poetic and peaceful moments – a fine, spring morning, for example, in the country or by the sea – seems so serene, so gentle, so calm, is in fact composed of a demonic destructive fury, even though that fury is completely hidden and absolutely invisible. Thus my inability to think the atomic fact does not arise from the imbalance between mass and energy, but from the idea of a harmless, lovable reality that can transform itself in an instant into an inferno. Or more exactly still, what amazes me is a sort of falseness and hypocrisy about nature, which, having apparently been conquered a thousand times, now rediscovers in an even more terrible fashion its ancient role as man's merciless enemy.

These reflections suddenly prompt an unexpected curiosity in a text where the end of the world is dealt with as something "thinkable"; *The Revelation of St John*. It is a bookish curiosity in the end, the curiosity of a relaxed, solitary reader in the small hours. And in fact the idea comes to me in the most superficial way when I suddenly put to myself the question: "At this point, why not take a look at what *Revelation* says? Who knows, maybe, in the blinding light of the atomic explosion those ancient pages will reveal something new and significant."

As you see, it is precisely the kind of otiose thought that sometimes comes to you at night when there's nothing to do but wait for the liberation of sleep in the company of a good book. But no sooner have I thought of *Revelation*, than I am seized by the impatient reflex of times gone by. It is the kind of impatience I used to feel as a boy when, dedicating my nights to a reading programme that was anything but otiose, I would suddenly jump out of my bed and run completely naked (I didn't wear vest or pyjamas then, either) to search through one of my father's hundreds of bookshelves for something I suddenly wanted to read.

I used to know my father's library like the back of my hand and would go straight to the place where the book was to be found. After the raid I'd go back to my room – the same room I have now – breathless, clutching my prey to my breast, and slip under the bedclothes again with the joy of the lover who's managed to bring the woman he loves to his bed.

Now, no sooner do I think of re-reading *Revelation* than I'm seized by the same impatience. I jump out of bed and go barefoot into the corridor, heading confidently towards the precise spot where, ever since I was a boy, my father, who is relatively ordered in his disorder, has always kept the books about religion on a shelf next to his study door.

I walk down the corridor with its twists and straight stretches and in the light of a rather dim lamp find the bookshelf next to the study door. The Bible is there, its black spine standing out from the other, lighter-coloured books. But as I'm reaching out to take it, I hear a confused sound of voices and realize that the study door is open a good hand's breadth. I stop and prick up my ears. Then, in the silence, I distinctly hear the following words, spoken by the at once authoritarian and gentle voice of my father: "Not like that, not like that, come on! Like in the photograph!"

To this sibylline phrase, another voice, which I immediately recognize as the nurse, Fausta's, answers equally gently, but without authority, on the contrary in a dependent, submissive tone: "But what photograph? There are so many." "The one where you're reading a book, come here, I'll show you." "But why? Can't you tell me without all this fuss?" "I'm telling you to come here." At this point I hear a faint sound, as of bare feet on a carpet. Then Fausta's drawling voice exclaims: "Oh, that one! But I can't do that position." "If you could do it for the photograph, you can do it for me too." "All right, but what if your son were to come, how would it look?" "It's two o'clock. Dodo will be asleep at this hour. Come on, take this book and go and put yourself on the armchair." "Okay, I'll do it. But remember, I'm only doing it to make you happy." "Of course, you're a good girl. You're doing it to make a poor old invalid happy, of course."

By the time my father comes out with this last remark, almost despite myself, and as though to confirm with my eyes what I've guessed through my ears, I already have my face to the crack of the door and am watching. Since the door is located in a corner of the study, I have only a partial view of the room. I can't see my father, nor the half of the room with the bed; but I do have an excellent view of the armchair at the foot of the bed where Fausta has just sat down. She is lying back a little; up top she's wearing her usual sloppy red sweater; from the waist down she's naked. She leans her head back on the armchair and looks at a book she's holding open a little way above her stomach. Beneath the book, in contrast to the chaste and thoughtful attention of the reader, her black crotch is incongruously displayed between open thighs, as though to attract another kind of attention. Fausta is small; her legs are thin; which makes the black fleece that covers her sex seem all the more enormous, fake almost, as though she were wearing a patch of bear or beaver fur.

There is a long silence. My father says nothing; obviously he's watching the spectacle of that extraordinary shagginess. For her part, the conscientious Fausta pushes her act so far as to turn a page of the book; at the same time she wriggles into a more comfortable position in the armchair, exactly as if settling down for a long, comfortable read. I can't help thinking that there's a curious and simultaneous interweaving of different kinds of looking going on: Fausta is looking at her book, my father is looking at that sort of bearish fur between her open legs and I am spying on Fausta and my father, even though I can't actually see the latter, to find out what kind of relationship has developed between them.

Finally my father's voice says: "Good. But now make a last little effort, let me really see it." "But haven't you seen enough?" "Come on, you know what I mean: really see it means see it open." "Oh, that's what you want, but then I'll have to have my hands free. I can't hold the book as well." "Chuck the book away then." "But they didn't make me do this for the photograph." "The photograph was for everybody, this is for me. Come on, I'm a poor invalid, it's as if you were doing me a good turn. Don't you want to do me a good turn?"

The words are spoken with unaccustomed and perhaps sincere pathos. Immediately afterwards I see Fausta put her book down with decision and move her hands to her crotch. At which I jerk violently back from the door. What's stopping me from going on watching? Not so much a belated sense of discretion, as the thought that I'm witnessing exactly the same kind of exhibitionism and voyeurism that I myself was involved in a few days ago in the Chinese restaurant. Like my father, I asked Silvia to show me her sex. Like Fausta, Silvia exhibited herself and was happy to be looked at. But now, seeing my father and the nurse doing what between Silvia and me had been an act of love, I find the thing so repugnant I can't look. It is the usual contradictory repulsion we feel at the thought of our own eroticism being acted out by others. But what makes it worse in this case is that the other person is my father, who, what's more, is the incarnation, as I see it, of everything I reject and condemn.

So I take the Bible from the shelf and without the joyous haste of the nocturnal raids of my adolescence, go slowly back to my room. I throw myself on the bed again and open the Bible at the pages of *Revelation*.

But a sudden thought distracts me, makes me put off my reading a while: given that my father and I resemble each other to the extent that we behave in the same way, in such a special relationship as that between voyeur and exhibitionist, why then do I go on hating him? Obviously because I recognized myself in him as though in a mirror, and didn't like the reflection I found there. But that's not the mirror's fault. So, I can't have it both ways: either I absolve the mirror and hence myself as well; or I condemn the mirror and again myself as well. There is, it's true, a third possibility: not to look at myself in the mirror and to go on hating my father not for the ways he's like me, but for the ways he isn't like me. Okay, but doesn't this momentary and partial similarity in our behaviours lead one to suspect other unforeseeable similarities in other areas? And, to be more straightforward, mightn't I perhaps be nothing more than an updated version of my father? A member of the same kind of society, but with the alibi of the protest movement?

All of a sudden I feel fed up with thinking about my father and go back to the Bible. I turn to the beginning of

Revelation and read through, stopping at all the places that seem most prophetic: "And the seven angels which had the seven trumpets prepared themselves to sound. The first angel sounded and there followed hail and fire mingled with blood," (the black rain after the explosion? The fallout?) "and they were cast upon the earth: and the third part of the trees was burnt up," (according to the calculations of the experts it would be two thirds, not one) "and all green grass was burnt up.

"And the second angel sounded, and as it were a great mountain burning with fire was cast into the sea:" (a multi-megaton bomb dropped in the sea by mistake?) "and the third part of the sea became blood; And the third part of the creatures which were in the sea, and had life, died; and the third part of the ships were destroyed." (A naval battle with nuclear weapons?)

"And the third angel sounded, and there fell a great star from heaven, burning as it were a lamp," (a space station hit by a laser ray?) "and it fell upon the third part of the rivers," (in Russia, or the USA?) "and upon the fountains of waters; And the name of the star is called Wormwood:" (exactly the kind of half-poetic, half-allusive name the military do give their weapons) "and the third part of the waters became wormwood," (radioactive pollution?) "and many men died of the waters because they were made bitter." (Radioactive, that is.) "And the fourth angel sounded," (but who are these angels, if not the political and military leaders safe in their supersonic aeroplanes? Or the nuclear scientists deep down in their underground shelters?) "and the third part of the sun was smitten, and the third part of the moon, and the third part of the stars; so as the third of them was darkened, and the day shone not for a third part of it, and the night likewise." (Perhaps the night caused by the so-called nuclear winter?)

As a description of nuclear war, this is certainly accurate, even if it is couched in the language of the time, dense with metaphors that are indeed apocalyptic; the explosion of a large number of medium-size, two-megaton bombs; the rain of dust and radioactive particles that follows; death by fire, by radioactivity, from hunger, from cold . . .

It has everything, both for the believer who takes the images of *Revelation* seriously, and likewise for the non-believer, like myself, who sees contemporary reality through those images. The only difference, I tell myself, between believer and non-believer is this: after St John's literary Apocalypse comes the kingdom of God; after the real apocalypse of today, zero.

Suddenly I've had enough of thinking about the end of the world too. I put down the Bible and, not without a sense of relief, go back to thinking about the scene of exhibitionism I witnessed a few minutes ago. Two details intrigue me: Fausta's acquiescence, all the more unexpected after her complaints about the liberties my father was taking with her; and then the mysterious allusions in their conversation to some photographs where Fausta appeared nude from the waist down with her legs spread.

The first mystery is easily explained by the reflection that in all probability Fausta hasn't changed her behaviour towards my father out of self-interest or servility, but simply as a result of that perhaps animal-like generosity I noticed previously in the emotional expression in her eyes. Yes, Fausta agreed to show my father her crotch to do him the good turn that he, hypocritically, had asked of her with fake and lecherous humility.

Which leaves the enigma of the photographs. Evidently there are some photographs somewhere showing Fausta in the same exhibitionist poses she adopted to please my father. Evidently my father knew of these photographs, had them in his hands in fact during the brief discussion that preceded the exhibition. But who took them? In what circumstances? Why? How did my father get hold of them? I can't answer these questions, but they do serve to spur my imagination. So I come up with a few ideas: the photographer is probably that ex-fiancé of hers, and very vain as fiancés often are. He probably photographed his girlfriend out of vanity. But why photograph her in an indecent pose? And then, why would Fausta have shown these photographs to my father? And finally, why did my father say the photographs had been taken for everyone? Amidst these and similar reflections, sleep finally gets the better of me and I drop off.

I don't know how long I sleep. Perhaps, as happens when one is both tired and wound up, not more than a few minutes, but with such intensity that on waking I feel as if I'd slept for hours. Completely lucid and rested, I wake up suddenly with the sensation that I'm not alone. And in fact I see Fausta sitting at the foot of the bed, motionless, watching me, as if she were waiting for me to wake.

Flustered, I ask: "What are you doing here?", not connecting her presence with the scene I watched a short while ago through the crack of the half-closed door.

Embarrassed, she replies: "I've been watching you sleep for quite a while. I didn't want to wake you, you were sleeping so soundly."

Now everything comes back: my search for the Bible, the door left ajar, my father's and Fausta's voices . . . I look around: the Bible has fallen to the floor, the lamp is still on. "Why did you come?"

She stares at me from those soft dark eyes of hers with their sly look, like a boy's, or a young hooligan's, rather: "Guess?"

Fed up, I say impatiently: "Yes, I know, because you saw me in the corridor. It's obvious. I was looking at you and you were looking at me. But what I'm asking you is, why did you come?"

"And you," she hits back boldly, "why did you go?"

It occurs to me that the words express the disappointment of the exhibitionist who, for some reason or other, has lost the attention of his or her voyeur. But I insist: "First of all you have to tell me why you came."

"Because," she explains ingenuously, "I didn't want you to think badly of me. I mean, I didn't do it for money or anything. I did it as a favour for your father. I swear."

"I know. You did it because you're generous."

She doesn't notice what I've said and goes on: "And then the other thing I thought was, he is a great man, he deserves it."

I'm surprised. I didn't expect this curious justification. "He deserves it?"

She doesn't answer, seems to be thinking it over. Then, a little uncertainly, as if my question had suddenly made her doubt my father's greatness, she says: "At least everybody says he's a great man."

I agree without reservations: "That's right, he is."

Bolstered up by my approval, she goes back on the offensive: "But what about you? Why did you leave?"

Sarcastically I finish: "At the juiciest moment, eh?"

With childish vanity she protests: "That part of my body is very beautiful. Everybody says so."

I hesitate, then decide to tell the truth: "Let's say I left so as not to do the same as my father."

She seems to understand, or rather pretends to. Ingenuously again, she exclaims: "You know why I did what your father wanted? Okay, this time I'll tell you. Because I realized you were watching me."

Thus, I can't help thinking, we have acted out the scene described in Mallarmé's poem: an erotic couple spied on by a chance observer. "Look," I object, "a few seconds ago you said you did it as a favour for him and because he's a great man. What's the truth?"

She shrugs her shoulders, throwing me a sly look of complicity: "What do you think?"

I say curtly: "I don't think anything. More to the point, what's all this about photographs, the ones my father wanted you to copy?"

She makes a mild gesture of impatience, as if this were a question of secondary importance that had been settled long ago: "Oh, the photographs. They're the ones in the magazine."

"What magazine?"

She mentions a title, one of the so-called "sexy mags". She explains: "They put a few photos of me in the thing. My fiancé took them – the photographer. We were going through a difficult patch, we didn't have any money, plus he said I could make a career as a model. So I agreed. I thought: who'll recognize me anyway? Afterwards, though, I wished I hadn't, because like I said we broke up and he didn't give me a penny. So when the people at the magazine wanted us to do another set, I told him no."

"But how come my father had a copy of the magazine?"

"I showed it to him. We were talking about this, that and the other and I told him the story of my engagement, so he asked to see the magazine and I gave it him. I thought he'd enjoy looking at it and that would be that. Instead, ever since he saw it, he's never stopped bothering me. He wanted me to pose for him, like in the photographs. So finally, tonight, I agreed." She hesitates, then asks: "Do you want to see the magazine?"

Caught off guard by this proposal, I say no more than: "How come you've got it here? You go round with it in your bag?"

Awkward, but sincere, she replies: "Sometimes I look through it myself. It's a souvenir, you know, like the photographs people take on holiday. And then, I didn't want to leave it at home. I was afraid Aunt Rita might see it."

A trifle bored, I say: "Why do you have to show me the magazine? I got a good enough look at you a few minutes back."

She objects: "You saw me in my, well, in my natural state. But the photographs are something else."

"That is?"

"Well, the photographs are artistic."

"Artistic?"

"Once artists used to paint their girlfriends. Now they do photographs, but it's the same thing."

I give in: "Okay, show me."

Delighted, she makes a dash for the door and disappears. A moment later she's back again, breathless with running, the magazine in her hand. Impetuously, she throws an arm round my shoulders while I leaf through it. "I'm in the middle," she explains happily. "They put me on the centre-page spread too, girl of the month."

And in fact, here is the centre-spread with Fausta lying face down, wearing a pullover, her bottom naked, her sweet, sly face turned toward the camera. On the other pages the pose is more or less the same as the one my father made her do a short while ago. Looking at the centre-spread, I say jokingly: "Anyone'd think you were waiting for someone to give you a vitamin shot."

She bursts into loud laughter, behind which I sense her relief at my easy-going attitude. Then she asks: "They are good, aren't they? I mean, artistic."

"Yes, they're artistic."

She sighs: "I said to your father: Don't ask for anything

more than a pose like in the photographs. But he's stubborn. He wanted more. The photographs were for everybody, he said, but I should do something specially for him. I told him, those artists who painted their girlfriends, they didn't show what they were like inside. They painted what you could see, as it was, normally, and that was that."

I mutter: "My father isn't an artist."

"I know. But what is he, then?"

"You said it yourself. A great man."

I close the magazine and give it back to her. She interprets my silence as a criticism and asks anxiously: "I don't look bad, do I?"

"No, on the contrary, you look marvellous."

She almost explodes with gratitude and asks impetuously: "Can I give you a kiss?"

And before I can answer she throws her arms round my neck and kisses me on the mouth.

I am struck by how huge Fausta's tongue is, and the thought of its size in proportion to her small body reminds me of the huge bush of her pubic hair. The tiny Fausta has a tongue as thick and rough as a calf's. She waggles it conscientiously into every recess of my mouth, then withdraws and says: "You know I like you."

I can't help asking: "Have you ever kissed my father like that?"

"You're joking, no kisses for him."

"So what am I supposed to make of your kiss?"

"Did you like it?"

"Yes."

"Think of it as a gift, like a bunch of flowers. But now I'd better be going. If your father finds out I'm here, there'll be trouble. You know he's jealous of you."

"Jealous of me?"

"Yes, the other day, while I was sponging him down,

you know what he said? He said, whose do you think is bigger, mine, or my son's?"

"And so, what did you say?"

"I ought to have said I didn't know, which would have been the truth. But then, to make him happy, I said I thought, of the two of you, he came out the winner. Well, I'm off, see you."

She hurries off and is gone. I'm left going over the meaning of the word "gift" that Fausta used to describe her kiss. I feel she's right; kissing me she meant to make me a present, the same way she meant to do my father a favour by exposing herself. A gift and a favour that didn't cost her anything, just like a bunch of flowers picked for free in the fields. Thinking it all over, I undress, climb under the covers and go straight to sleep.

CHAPTER EIGHT

The Blow

❧

I'm sitting in the armchair at the foot of my father's bed. On my knees I've got the newspaper I just went to get from the kiosk down in the street. I'm watching my father sleeping. Usually he's awake when I arrive, waiting for his breakfast, sitting up against the pillows, already well-groomed, even if he hasn't had his wash yet. But this morning everything's different. I wasn't able to pick up the breakfast tray in the kitchen. Fausta wasn't there, the light was off and the room dark. Probably she's out buying yoghurt and bread. And then for the first time since his accident, my father was still asleep. So I decided to let him be.

From the armchair I can see his head in profile, resting on one side on the pillow with that relaxed, vulnerable look, typical of sleep and death. Without paying particular attention, I look at his tousled hair, his protruding, bristling eyebrows, the imperious nose with the nostrils visible from below, the mouth, which in sleep seems set in an expression nearer disgust than disdain. Finally my gaze settles on his cheek, or rather on a small, light-coloured wart near his ear. When I was a boy, I would often watch my father while he shaved and be struck by how carefully he would slide the blade over the wart, making sure not to cut himself. But the real reason for my present interest in that tiny growth lies elsewhere. As I watch my father's drawn, yet for all that, red cheek, I realize that, unexpectedly and absurdly, I feel an impulse to strike him in the face. But the really odd thing about this temptation is that it seems divorced from any feeling of hostility. If anything it seems inexplicably linked to something that happened in the past, something I've already done. But what?

I try to remember but can't think of anything. The link is there, but it's holed up in the darkest recesses of my memory and won't come out. Then another unusual thing happens in this unusual morning. The door that leads from the study to the adjoining bedroom where Fausta sleeps, opens, and the nurse appears.

I realize at once that she must have only just got up. True, she's wearing her usual outfit, a red sweater and blue jeans, but she seems dazzled and muddled. On seeing me, she runs a hand through tousled hair to tidy it. Then in a tone of unpleasant surprise, she asks: "What on earth's the time?"

I tell her. So then she comes up beside me and, indicating my father with a glance, whispers: "Let him sleep, he needs it. I'll go and get the bread."

I can't help asking: "Were you up late last night?"

She replies quickly: "Certainly were. Really late. Three o'clock."

"But why?"

She gestures impatiently: "Let me get on out. We'll talk about it later," and she hurries off.

I'm left alone, wondering what that, "We'll talk about it later," means. Then, curiously, my attempt to understand what lies behind Fausta's reticence, serves to dislodge the block in my memory. The reason for my mysterious impulse to hit my father in the face as he sleeps floats to the surface. I'd sensed that it must have something to do with something that happened in the past, something I'd done. Now I remember exactly what it was I did and when.

As a boy, in a moment of bad temper, I hit my father. It was a weak, clumsy blow I'm sure, but in the heat of the moment it seemed like a violent, even desecrating thump. It's not easy now, after so many years, to define the strange feeling, half-remorse, half-fear, that this unheard-of act of filial rebellion aroused in me at the time. And then, that's not what I'm trying to remember now. What I want to know is why, a few minutes ago, I felt the same identical impulse on seeing my sleeping father's cheek.

I try to remember what happened in detail and discover to my amazement that everything comes back to me immediately with the precision peculiar to those experiences you've never forgotten nor put behind you. I think I must have been between seven and nine years old when it happened. My father and mother (Mother was to die some three years later of a mysterious illness that I now know was cancer of the uterus) had what must be a very common relationship between a modest woman past her prime and a brilliant man at the height of his virility and success. My father had ceased to love her, if indeed he had ever loved her; he neither slept with her nor went out with her in the evening; he was out all day except for siesta time, but then he didn't want to be disturbed. At the time of this episode, what I remember most clearly about my mother is her physical presence, in which, as one can well imagine, I caught hints not only of her character but also of the kind of relationship she had with my father. It is as if she were here before me now: a woman no longer young and in an indefinable way, desperate; blonde, her face a shade long and horsey with small, deep-set, intensely blue eyes, the nose upturned, the mouth big and sensual. Tall and very thin, bony even, her lanky body had, like a dried-up tree with the odd ripe fruit on its branches, unforeseen rotundities: the heavy hanging breasts, the marked oval of the buttocks, the big, misshapen calves. For my father it was probably a marriage of convenience; my mother came from a wealthy if not exactly rich family. But I remember her as a dependent, anxious person. Her money hadn't given her any security in her relationship with her husband.

Was she a good mother, my mother? What I remember most of all about her was a somehow pathetic way she had of expressing her maternal love. Every morning, very early, she would come to wake me up and open the window. She would burst impetuously into the room in her dressing gown, cross to the window in the dark, open it and then lean out over the sill to throw open the shutters. Making this energetic movement, her dressing gown inevitably came undone at the front, so that she appeared in the sudden daylight to my still sleep-blurred eyes in a transparent pink or pale-blue cotton nightdress, all crumpled up, through which I could distinctly see her swinging breasts bouncing against her ribcage. With that sense of decorum typical of the child, I was shocked, not by the nudity at all but by the untidiness. I would have been happier if she'd come to wake me dressed to the nines. Often I was on the point of saying: "What do you come in your nightie for? Why don't you get dressed first?" But I didn't, held back by I don't know what feeling of shyness mingled with compassion. Why I should have felt compassion for her, I couldn't have said. Perhaps because of the anxious energy with which she leaned out over the windowsill every morning. Perhaps because I sensed in this violence the desperate desire of the neglected wife to compensate for the inadequacy of conjugal love with her maternal love.

At that time, like so many children of my age, I used to collect stamps. Faced with my passion as a collector, my father and mother responded very differently. My mother, who didn't know anything about the subject, frequently gave me stamps, but ones I either had already or didn't want because they were too common. My father, on the contrary, did know about stamps, but often, out of carelessness, he would forget to give me any. To make up for this, there was a tacit understanding between us that every time he got a letter from abroad, he would keep the stamps for me. Despite his carelessness, my father had so far kept to this.

One day it so happened that I caught sight of a yellow envelope on my father's desk with a lot of big, colourful stamps on it – Vatican City I think they were. Now, whether it was that my father had forgotten our understanding for once, or whether – as seems more likely – he wanted to hang on to the envelope so as to be able to answer the letter that was in it, the fact is that quite a few days went by and "my" stamps were still there on his desk, all the more desirable because visible. What to do? I realized that the simplest strategy would be to speak directly to my father and ask him for the stamps; but I didn't want to do that out of a sense of – how can I put it? – propriety. Was there or was there not a tacit understanding between myself and my father over the stamps on his letters? And if there was, wouldn't a request on my part perhaps give my father the impression I didn't trust him? In the end I settled on a compromise. I wouldn't ask my father for the stamps directly. I'd have my mother ask him for me.

So one hot afternoon in June, come siesta time – the only time I could be sure my father would be home – I went to look for my mother in her bedroom. Normally I'd have gone in without knocking, but that day the unusual nature of my visit made me behave in an unusual way. So, I knocked timidly and, not getting a reply, knocked again, louder. Then I heard my mother's voice say: "Oh, it's you, hang on a minute." The tone of her voice was at once surprised and joyous, a tone which, had I not been blinded by philatelic passion, I certainly wouldn't have attributed to my visit. But I just thought she was telling me not to come in. So I waited for what seemed a strangely long time until, impatient and shrill, she shouted: "You can come in now, come on in."

At first glance, seeing her standing in the middle of the room feverishly tying the belt of a short, white towelling jacket, I appreciated my mistake: my mother had mistaken me for someone else, my father obviously. And then as soon as she saw me she confirmed my suspicion by saying: "Oh, but it's you," where that "but" stood for nothing if not a sense of disappointment.

For a moment I was almost tempted to tell her any old lie I could and get out. But I wanted those stamps too badly. So, in an irritated, reproachful voice, I quickly explained why I'd come, taking care to stress that the stamps in question were already practically mine and that all she had to do was to remind my father of my right to have them, a right consecrated in the past by other, similar gifts. Bit by bit, as I was talking, I saw my mother's face, which only a moment ago had looked cross, go from disappointment to an attentive and, so it seemed, calculating expression. Finally she came close to me and, stroking my hair, gentle and doubtful, asked affectionately: "Do you want your stamps right now, or would you rather I talked

to Daddy this evening? He'll be resting now, he won't want
to be disturbed."

Instinctively I understood that my mother was presenting me with a false dilemma, that that "this evening"
was suggested only to save an appearance of respect for
my father's siesta. The fact was, I sensed, that my mother
had her own reasons for wanting me to take upon myself
the responsibility for disturbing my father's sleep. So that
in the face of this ill-concealed encouragement it wasn't hard
for me to reply in a loud voice: "I want them now!"

My mother's hand lingered on my head, her fingers
slipping into the hair over my forehead, ruffling it. With a
question in her voice, she repeated: "So, you want them
now, do you?" And after a moment: "Very well, I'll go and
ask him for them. A yellow envelope on the desk, you said?
Wait for me here, perhaps I can get it without waking
him." So saying, at a strangely quick, almost dancing pace,
she left the room.

Of course, as soon as she'd gone, I disobeyed her and,
though keeping my distance so she wouldn't catch on, I
followed her. She went ahead of me down the corridor,
walking smartly with that towelling jacket dancing above
her calves, animated by a boldness that I sensed had
nothing to do with me. Finally, I saw her stop in front of
the study door, wait a moment without knocking and then,
very very slowly, turn the handle, as if she really did mean
to take the envelope without waking my father. Then she
opened the door and, going in, left it ajar behind her, apparently intending to leave immediately and without making
any noise.

I realize at this point in my journal, that my life may
seem full of doors left ajar. But that's not so. The only door
truly left ajar in my life, now I come to think of it, was
the door to my father's study in that remote and sultry

June afternoon of twenty-seven years ago. After that afternoon my feelings for my father would never be the same again. I could almost say that I no longer thought of him as my father.

So I found the door left ajar and waited a while. My mother had told me she would take the envelope from the table without waking my father; which meant the whole thing shouldn't take more than a minute or two. But the wait went on much longer than expected. I waited and waited, counting the seconds and minutes, and then in the end I gave the door a slight push, just enough to be able to see into the room.

The desk was placed, as it still is, to the left of the door, so I looked there first to see what had happened to my stamps. Which was when I saw what looked like a decapitated head on the desktop, its body outside my angle of vision. This head, forced fiercely down against the desk, was my mother's; my father's hand was squeezing her neck, holding her tight in that position at once so strange and so uncomfortable. All I could see of my father was part of his arm; but this was enough for me to realize that he was behind her, bearing down on her and forcing her to bend over the desk. The idea of violence, a violence inexplicably accepted and unopposed, was suggested not only by my mother's unnatural position, but also by the expression on her face, which was precisely that of a decapitated head immediately after the execution, with eyes open and staring, and a mouth set in a now silent shriek. With the logic of a child, I imagined my father was inflicting something like a punishment on my mother; but at the same time I sensed a mysterious complicity on her part. She wasn't struggling; and it occurred to me that the hand that kept her nailed to the desk was unnecessary: my mother would have stayed bent down there even without it.

I saw, thought and felt all this in just a split second.

Then, tense and panting, my father's voice broke the silence: "Go on then, tell me you're my pig, tell me, or I'll break your neck." In response to this command, the severed head stuttered meekly in a laboured voice: "Yes, you know I am, you know I'm your pig." "Say it again." But this time, instead of obeying, the head broke out in a long plaintive groan, as if in intolerable pain. Frightened, I drew back from the door.

But it wasn't just the spectacle of that severed martyr's head that made me run off. There was also an element of calculation springing from my childish greed. Because, while groaning and crushed beneath my father's weight, my mother had her arm bent across the desk, her hand close to her mouth. And in that hand she was still clutching, as I could quite clearly see, the large yellow envelope with the Vatican City stamps.

Thinking back on it now, I would explain that envelope held tightly in my mother's fist during their love-making as follows: my mother went into the study; my father saw her from where he was lying on the divan, suddenly felt he wanted her and grabbed her just as she took hold of the envelope, the transparent pretext for her visit.

But at the time I wasn't thinking of the real reason why my mother, like a castaway swept off by a wave, should be holding on to that envelope as if on to something precious that must at all costs be saved from their conjugal violence. My only thought was that my mother had kept her promise after all and that all I had to do now was go back to her room and wait for her there.

So I sneaked off on tip-toe. But then, I don't know why, I went past my mother's door and took refuge in my own room. I sat down at my little table and started to flick mechanically through my stamp album. Why didn't I go and wait for my mother in her room as she'd told me to?

Perhaps because I suddenly realized that she had used my plea for help to further her own ends, and I was ashamed of having asked her.

I waited a long time; then the noise of the door opening behind me warned me that she'd finished with my father and was coming to bring me the envelope. But I didn't turn round. I wanted to give her the impression that I didn't care now whether I got the stamps or not. Then I heard someone coming up behind me with a different step from my mother's, and at the same time my father's voice said: "I've brought your stamps, Dodo, here." So then I turned and saw him, smiling kindly, holding out the yellow envelope still all crumpled from the convulsed grip of my mother's hand.

I don't know to this day what came over me then. I said brusquely: "I don't want them any more," and I swiped a great blow at my father's hand. But just as I hit out, he bent down towards me, so that instead of hitting his hand, my swipe caught him full in the face, on his cheek. My father was unruffled, of course. He exclaimed coolly, though not without surprise: "How rude!" Then he put the stamps on the bedside table and went off.

At that point my memory goes blank. What did I do with the stamps? Did I think over what had happened later? How did I feel towards my father and mother? What happened between us when we all three saw each other again that evening at dinner? How did my father and mother behave towards me? I don't remember anything, nothing at all. Obviously I had been, as it were, dazzled by the truth, and like someone who thinks he's seen something unbelievable, but isn't entirely sure, I had instinctively put off the search for some kind of assurance to a calmer, less disturbed moment in the future. But what I do remember very well is the sensation I had the following morning when my mother came as usual to throw open the shutters. While she was opening the window and leaning out over the sill to fasten the two heavy shutters on their hooks, her movements full of that pathetic energy of hers, her dressing gown flew open as it did every day, and once again I saw her bony body through the transparent nightdress with those big hanging breasts that bounced on her ribcage. So far, as I said before, my mother's unintentional nudity had aroused the sort of embarrassment you feel at somebody's wearing the wrong kind of clothes. But that morning, I'm sure, I must have connected her nudity to the scene I'd glimpsed in my father's study, and for a moment my embarrassment was replaced by a feeling I'd never had before, a feeling of cruel curiosity. This was my mother then, but was she also the woman I'd seen bent over my father's desk, the woman I'd heard come out with that strange insult against herself? I must have had a very different expression in my eyes just then from the one I normally had. My mother noticed, threw me a sidelong glance and with a sweep of her hand closed the dressing gown. But this happened only that one day. Every other morning, the same unintentional exhibition went on as before, as though she'd forgotten that new expression of mine. But then, I'd forgotten it too. I'd gone back to watching her without curiosity or cruelty, but with the same childish embarrassment at her untidiness that I'd felt in the past.

This, then, is the memory that comes back to me, sharply focused and well organized, with all its colours and gestures, as I watch my father sleep. Then, with the sensation of making an important discovery, I remember how, a few days ago at the Chinese restaurant, to justify her "crush" on this other man, Silvia said she wasn't a madonna, as I insisted on thinking of her, but a pig. And "pig" was the same word my mother panted out twenty-seven years before in response to my father's command: "Yes," she said, "I am your pig."

It does not immediately occur to me to trace back the similarity of the words spoken so many years apart to a single source. Perhaps the truth blinds me, like the headlights of a car that's running me down. At first I'm struck by the similarity and nothing else; then a little later I exclaim to myself: "But it's obvious, the word 'pig' was spoken by my mother twenty-seven years ago and by Silvia just a few days back for the very same reason, which is that my father likes to hear it said." I stop thinking for a few moments. Then clinch it: "And in exactly the same position, making love with both of them from behind, the animal way. With my mother I know because I saw her; with Silvia because she told me herself."

Oddly enough, while a few minutes ago, when I still hadn't guessed at or pieced together the truth of his relationship with Silvia, I was tempted to strike my father in the face; now that I'm quite sure, I seem to be watching him without any urge to be violent. It's as if my violence had been tied up with my blindness, a blindness followed now by a clairvoyance that may be appalled, but which remains, at bottom, resigned in the face of this new and for the moment unbelievable fact: my father is my wife's lover.

But there is something else which decides me against violence. Now that I think of it, if I were to hit my father, I would cease to behave like a son and become nothing more than Silvia's husband. For his part, he would cease to be my father and become no more than a rival in love. And a successful rival at that. Because there's no doubt that, at least for the moment, Silvia prefers to be treated as a pig rather than a madonna. In short, our whole father/son relationship would degenerate into a contest between two males for the possession of a female – a way of looking at the situation which, aside from anything else, is characteristic only of my father (I haven't forgotten the way he showed off his penis during the injection rite). I, on the other hand, want his connection with Silvia to keep its incestuous nature, and this because, while I can't really blame a successful rival for having stolen my woman, I can at least think that my father, if for no other reason than out of self-respect, should have refrained from going to bed with my wife.

I realize that this desire to see the father rather than the male in my rival derives, and not very unconsciously either, from the relationship my father has established with Silvia, a relationship in which I sense a profanatory cruelty directed, via Silvia, at myself. Yes, it's me my father wants to offend somehow by having Silvia *more ferarum*; it's me he wants to insult by having her call herself his "pig". And then, this isn't just his way of seeing our situation: it's mine too, because while he aims to insult and offend his rebellious, dissenting son through his relationship with his daughter-in-law, I in turn insult and offend him by considering him as nothing more than a representative figure of the society I'm rebelling against.

But this is all words. The fact remains that my father is Silvia's lover. Confronted with this statement, my mind fills with sharp images and bizarre ideas. I remember my mother bent at right angles over the desk while my father bore down on her and penetrated her from behind, and I tell myself that very probably I was conceived in the same position. Or I imagine Silvia making love with her father-in-law and ask myself ironically: if Silvia gets pregnant by my father, then as well as passing for my child, won't the baby she has be my brother too? And apart from being my wife, won't Silvia be my mother as well, or rather my step-mother? But irony isn't going to get me anywhere: the truth is, I'm hurting like a dog at the thought that my father has done with Silvia what twenty-seven years ago he did with my mother.

Finally I tell myself that in reality I don't want to accept and indeed am incapable of accepting the new relationship created between my father and myself by the discovery of his relationship with Silvia. Life is a question of relationships, not moral judgements; and you pretty soon have to realize that a new relationship alters all the others that came before it. This thought calms me down. I look at my father's head resting on the pillow and decide that what I must do first of all is discover what kind of feeling I have for him at precisely the moment he wakes up, opens his eyes and looks at me. It's a bit like tossing a coin, I admit, but there you are. I can't go on obsessively imagining Silvia doing and saying, after so many years, what my mother did and said in the past.

I've barely reached this conclusion when my father opens his eyes and looks at me. He looks at me for a long time, longer than I can bear. Then in a decisive voice, as if he hadn't been sleeping up to now, but only pretending, so that in fact he's already thought what to say, he says: "I know perfectly well that you can't stand me, so what are you doing here?"

The words provoke a complicated, very nasty feeling in me. What my father says is true, but it's a minimal truth compared with the one I could level at him. Still, precisely because he got in first, he has prevented me from turning the accusation back at him. On the other hand, despite the coldness and decision in his voice, I did sense some kind of pain there. It is clear that my father is afraid I may hate him. But this gives rise to another question: is he afraid I hate him because he thinks I know about his affair with

Silvia, or because he's aware of my, as it were, social hatred? Impossible to find out without starting an argument that would be loathsome. In any case, it is also clear that my father doesn't want me to tell him the truth. He just wants me to stop defying him; or, if I do know about his affair with Silvia, to forgive him, or rather, not to attach any importance to the matter. Which, when you get down to it, is a veiled way of forgiving.

So, in the end, my father has achieved his goal: my feeling for him remains a filial one. But wasn't that what I wanted, too? Given that there's such complete, albeit unintentional, agreement between us, all I can do is deny, deny everything.

With a reasonable degree of sincerity I exclaim: "What on earth are you talking about, Dad? What an idea!"

Quick as can be, the way a man in the water will grab the rope that's thrown to him, my father accepts my protest. "God knows why one thinks these things sometimes! I woke up, saw you watching me in a different sort of way and so . . ."

"But what way? I was waiting for you to wake up."

He immediately changes the subject: "Forget it, forget it. By the way, what time is it? I was up late last night watching television."

I tell him. He remarks: "The physiotherapist will be here soon. He should be bringing some crutches: it seems I'm supposed to try and walk."

With forced cheerfulness, I say: "Why 'supposed to'? You're bound to be able to walk, thank God."

"Okay, let's say I'll walk."

His voice has a strange, humbled, painful inflexion to it. "Why?" I ask him. "Aren't you pleased?"

He thinks for a moment, then says: "So long as I was in bed, I felt better somehow, more sure of myself, stronger.

God knows why, but my bed gave me strength, inspired some kind of hope that I would recover, not just from the fracture, but from another problem too."

"What's that?"

"Old age."

I take a quick look at him. Suddenly he seems thin, worn-out, exhausted. I say: "But you're not old."

"Of course I am. But knowing he's going to get better tends to fool an old man. As long as he's in bed, he imagines that not only will he recover from the problem he's got, but that he'll rediscover other powers as well."

"What powers?"

He looks at me, as though to see if I still hate him, or if I'm feeling friendly. He must be reassured by what he finds because he says with simplicity: "Intellectual powers, for example; sexual powers, too."

"What do you mean?"

There's a sudden jolt in my voice, perhaps because I wasn't expecting my father to tackle so explicitly a subject that will inevitably lead me back to Silvia. He answers with sudden, unexpected confidence: "I mean that while I've been bed-ridden I've aroused a kind of interest in some of my female visitors that I could never have dreamt of arousing when I was in good health."

He is silent, then goes on, as though thinking out loud: "Heaven only knows why women find a patient lying in his bed under the sheets so exciting!"

"And so?"

"And so the patient gets illusions about himself and his own sexual capacities."

All of a sudden, gripped by a terrifying suspicion, I ask: "During these last three months that you've been in bed, excuse my asking, but have you had any, well, to be frank, any adventures?"

His profile is towards me now and he doesn't turn. He answers in a neutral, impersonal voice: "I don't know what you call adventures. Let's say that, despite the accident, or rather perhaps because of it, I've had some luck."

I hesitate, then make up my mind: "But isn't it difficult to make love in bed with a fractured thigh?"

He shakes his head: "No, it isn't. Partly because these dear ladies who come to visit their old sick professor have such diabolical courage. They aren't satisfied with furtive petting; even when the door is open and there is the danger of someone coming in and seeing them, they're quite capable of hiking up their dresses and jumping on the bed."

I can't help seeing Silvia, her legs spread, skirts pulled up, standing on my father's bed. With an effort, I get out: "Yes, women do have a lot of courage."

This time he doesn't answer. I wait for him to go on with his erotic confidences, partly out of a malevolent desire to see him slip into vulgarity, something that so far he has managed, without realizing it, to avoid; partly in an attempt to recognize Silvia in one of these "diabolically courageous" visitors. But at the same time the ambivalent feeling I have for my father makes me hope that he won't fall into the trap of vulgarity, and again that the spectre of Silvia will not emerge from his descriptions. Meanwhile, my father seems to reflect, then says in an urbane, benevolent voice: "Don't you think the subject is a shade unsuitable for father and son?"

With ambiguous sincerity, I reply: "You're right. I don't know why, but sometimes I find myself forgetting that you're my father."

With an odd courage he answers: "I don't see what else I could be if not your father."

I'm on the point of exclaiming: "My rival, Silvia's lover!", but stop myself. With conscious flattery I insist: "It's strange, but I'm always forgetting the age-gap between us."

"Unfortunately," he points out ironically, "I can't forget it."

With a clear reference to his relationship with Silvia, I object: "The fact is, there are times when I think of you as a contemporary, someone who could quite easily be my own rival in love."

He doesn't pick up the allusion. Looking into the air, he says: "And instead, I'm an old man." He falls silent a moment, then adds: "An old man who sometimes suffers from the illusion that he's young."

I say nothing, waiting. He goes on: "There are times when I want to say to these women who delude me and delude themselves: but can't you see that I'm almost a corpse already? That my skin is wasted, my muscles powerless, my legs spindly, my stomach flabby, eyes sunken? What on earth do you see in me?"

His tone is more peevish than bitter, irritated almost. I try to console him: "Women don't care about that kind of thing."

"So what do they care about?"

I would like to be offensive and unfair and tell him: "About the thing you were flaunting a few days ago when Fausta was giving you your injection." But I realize I'm not going to say what I think; no, I'm going to say what he was thinking on that occasion. I tell him pompously: "Everyone needs vitality, but women need it more than men: all they care about is vitality. And you appear to have it."

Then we both fall silent. Now, confronted with my father's bitterness, I realize I'm wasting my time: I'll never manage to work it so that I feel entirely indifferent towards him, which is the only feeling, or rather lack of it, I'd like to have in his regard. The fundamental question, though, is whether I really want to know if Silvia is his lover or not. What if there were no truth at all in my assumption? If my reconstruction of their relationship based entirely on that single word "pig" pronounced twenty-seven years ago by my mother and repeated by Silvia just a few days back, were only the merest coincidence? If, in short, I were becoming, without realizing it, the kind of jealous character who prefers to be mistakenly certain of betrayal rather than properly uncertain?

I think hard. Once again I go over the clues, all of them psychological, unfortunately. So, I would seem to be the man Silvia loves, the man of her life; for the man she is betraying me with, she merely has what she calls a "crush". She'd like to break off with this man, but every time she sees him she ends up back where she started again, because he makes love in a way that is new and irresistible for her. For his part, the man she betrays me with would also like to end the affair, but he too can't help getting involved again, obviously because ... I stop here, suddenly struck by a simple truth: there is only one man in the world who, despite being strongly attracted to Silvia, could nevertheless feel he ought to break off with her, and that man is my father.

So, it's no good trying to fool myself that nothing has happened between my father and my wife. Which leaves me with the dilemma of whether I should give up trying to find out the truth and wait passively for the "crush" to finish of its own accord; or whether I should try to find out more, find out everything in fact. One simple reflection inclines me towards the first course: what is the point of my finding out, since I have no intention of giving up Silvia, since I love her and would certainly continue to love her even if she told me she had no intention of breaking off with my father? But, oddly, it is precisely my love which makes me decide for the opposite course of action: I must know, and know everything, because only in this way will I put my feeling for her to the test, will I know if I really love Silvia.

But if I'm to know everything, shouldn't I start with my father? Yes, I should, even though I find the idea of talking to him about Silvia, even indirectly, profoundly repugnant. I decide to make an effort.

"Don't you think there may be more vitality in the person who stops in time, rather than in the person who lets himself go completely? I mean, there's a great deal of vitality in desire; but perhaps there's even more in renunciation."

My father seems to have recovered from the momentary depression of a few minutes before that prompted such sincerity on the subject of old age. He sends me an inquiring look, then asks: "How come there's no breakfast today?"

"You slept really late and so did Fausta. I think she's gone down to get the bread. So? Aren't you going to answer my question?"

Curiously, he doesn't avoid the confrontation. He says immediately, but thoughtfully: "Basically you're asking me whether it's right to hold back in love, to renounce. And my answer is this: it may well be right, but no one has ever held themselves back without regretting it later."

So, I can't help thinking, there we are, I got what I asked for. My father, no doubt about it, understood the underlying meaning of my spiel on vitality and is giving me my answer in like fashion. I watch him with eyes that must seem unnaturally staring because he adds: "In the end you think the same way I do."

I'd like to yell: "So it's not true, what Silvia says, that

you agree with her about wanting to end the affair. So you want to go on, all the way." But I only manage to come out with a stupid: "Not exactly. Still, no one could deny that you do have very clear ideas."

Can my father see the pain I'm in? Apparently so, because he adds quietly: "Of course, one can hold back in love, renounce. But this simply means that vitality doesn't manage to get the better of boredom. That is, that one doesn't love enough."

"Or that one isn't vital enough perhaps?"

"There are all sorts of possibilities. There are the collectors – Don Juan, for example, was a collector – the kind who think: I still haven't had, let's say, a brunette with blue eyes. So they look for one, find her and then once they've added her to their collection, they lose interest."

I'm on the point of exclaiming: "Your collection was short of a rare example wasn't it? Your son's wife, your daughter-in-law." Instead I say in a teacherly voice: "Don Juan wasn't a collector. He was a power merchant."

My father searches my face, obviously trying to decide if I'm still alluding to him. Then he asks: "In what way?"

"The simplest and most direct way possible: the one that prompts us to seek confirmation of our existence through having power over others. In Don Juan's case, over women."

He says carelessly: "Could be. But the fact remains that a lot of men simply want to be in a position to say to themselves: I laid that woman. In such cases it is possible to renounce, certainly. But that's not love."

So he lets me know not only that he has made love with Silvia, but also that he doesn't love her and that he had an affair with her simply to be able to say afterwards: I laid her. I'm aware of being horribly humiliated by my father's contempt for Silvia. I realize with a feeling of rage that I'd have preferred it if he really did love her. So, I think, while I'm feeling desperate, they're about to break off their affair out of a sort of satiated boredom. Silvia has exhausted the novelties of love *alla more ferarum* and my father can now happily tell himself he's laid his daughter-in-law as well as all the others. Yet again my father seems to guess what I'm thinking because he winds up: "Some women give all they're capable of the first time. And once you've satisfied your curiosity, what's left?" I reply: "Meat without the salt."

Meat without salt! Silvia's body, meat without salt! Silvia's beauty, at once spiritual and sensual, mysteriously ambiguous, compared to a tasteless steak! My Byzantine madonna reduced to something on a butcher's slab! I feel, as I said, humiliated, and what is more, humiliated at feeling humiliated. Then, suddenly, the conversation takes yet another twist, and my father concludes unexpectedly: "But come to think of it, you can also renounce love precisely because it has been too wonderful and you want to conserve the memory intact, before the wonder turns into boredom or worse. Yes, that's another possibility."

What's got a hold of me? I want to grab my father's hand now and kiss it with warmth and gratitude. Yes, because with that remark on love he has said two, for me, very important things: first, that his relationship with Silvia has been "too wonderful"; second, that he will give up the affair precisely because it was so wonderful. Oh, but how much filial self-abasement there is in this gratitude of mine!

Just then, a baritone voice from the far end of the study asks: "May I?"

My father raises his eyes and says in a resigned voice: "Come in, come in."

It is Osvaldo, the little physiotherapist with the bald skull and handlebar moustache. He comes in holding out a pair of shining metal crutches, the kind you have to strap to your forearms. His attitude is at once triumphant and false, though being both professional-sounding and flattering the falseness is well suited to the task of pleasing my father: "Good morning, Professor, good morning. Great day today, Professor. A new life! We're going to start walking again."

My father looks at him doubtfully, as if the little man were announcing the success of some improbable scientific experiment. "I really am afraid I won't manage it. Yesterday I tried to put a foot on the floor and honestly, my head spun. Strange, because while I was in bed I felt like a lion!"

Osvaldo exclaims pompously: "One gets attached to everything, even one's bed. But have no fear, Professor. Now, you get up and we'll take a little turn around the house, we'll go and say hello to Miss Fausta in the kitchen."

"But I'm not even dressed yet."

"You don't have to get dressed. You can take a walk in your pyjamas. A new life, Professor, a new life."

The little man approaches the bed, leans the crutches against the armchair, and makes to pull away the bedclothes. My father moves quickly to stop him: "No, hang on, what are you trying to do?"

"Take away the covers and make you walk through the house in your pyjamas." At this point there follows a scene without words, a scene that lasts no more than a few seconds perhaps, but that seems to me both long and obscurely significant. My father looks at me, he looks at the little man, he looks at his own body lying under the covers. Finally he says: "All right, we'll take a little walk. But at least let me put on some fresh pyjamas. Dodo, please, go and get me some pyjamas, they're in Fausta's room."

I get up and ask: "Where exactly?"

For a moment my father watches me in silence as if not remembering where the pyjamas are. Then he says curtly: "In the dresser, top drawer."

I cross to the door of the room where Fausta sleeps and go in. Before his accident this was my father's bedroom. It is square with a very high ceiling and Empire-style furniture: a bed, a dresser, a cupboard with bronze columns and capitals, a few chairs with lyre-shaped backs. The bed where Fausta slept last night is still unmade, the covers thrown back, as if to suggest the bounce of the nurse's young body as she leapt out. A ray of sunshine comes in through the windows, brightening the yellow-and-green striped material used for chairs and coverlet alike. I open the top drawer of the dresser and there are his pyjamas, two rows of them, carefully ironed and folded. I choose a nut-brown coloured pair, close the drawer, then suddenly stop still, because through the open door to the study comes the sound of my father's voice talking to Osvaldo: "I was hot in the night and it seems I must have kicked off my trousers in my sleep. Yes, look where they've gone and ended up."

I hear Osvaldo answer in his flattering voice: "Barely April and it's hot as June." This is a total lie, because it's actually a fairly cold April with frequent thunderstorms. After a brief glance in the mirror over the dresser at my anxious face (but anxious about what? Why?), I go back into the study.

Osvaldo is standing near the bed. From where I am, my father, stretched on the undersheet with nothing over him and naked from the waist down, appears in a dramatic foreshortening reminiscent of Mantegna's Christ. But the resemblance to the famous picture doesn't distract me from a sudden suspicion. It seems clear that my father asked me, rather than Osvaldo, to go and get his pyjamas because he didn't want me to see him naked when the phy-siotherapist pulled away the bedclothes. And this because he was ashamed, not so much of being naked, but of the absence of his pyjama trousers, which, in fact, I can now make out. They are not pushed down towards his feet, as they would be if he had wanted to kick them off because of the heat, but bundled up under his buttocks to relieve another kind of discomfort – and I've a shrewd idea which. As I come back into the room, Osvaldo is pulling the trousers out from under him and my father arches his back and lifts his buttocks to help. Seeing this reinforces the obsessive image I have of Silvia helping my father to get his trousers off his legs, while he, in a frenzy of desire, slips them under his backside.

Yes, Silvia came to see him last night; that's why my father woke up so late; and now, out of a belated sense of guilt, having triumphed once again over his own wavering conscience and her inept resistance, he can hardly help but feel ashamed on seeing me.

I go straight over to him and hand him the pyjamas, saying: "Are these okay?"

My father nods. He seems embarrassed, though I can't understand why. Then I notice that he's looking down at his crotch, and it occurs to me that maybe he had an orgasm during the night, and he realizes that there's a visible difference between the penis that's hot for it and the penis that's had it. Osvaldo says: "There we are Professor, lift your feet a little." My father obeys and Osvaldo quickly slips on his new pyjama-trousers. Then the jacket. Finally, Osvaldo says: "Now, Professor, turn round on the bed, move into a sitting position and put your feet on the floor. Like that, good. Now try to get up."

My father is on his feet beside the bed in his nut-brown

pyjamas with cream-coloured lapels, the trousers too long, hiding his feet. Dazed and apparently tired even before he has started, he brushes a hand over his head to tidy hair that has no need for it. The physiotherapist hands him the crutches. "Now, Professor, lean on the crutches and try to move your legs."

"But my head's spinning!"

"It doesn't matter, that's quite normal, you haven't walked for three months. Getting started is the main thing. Tomorrow you'll walk round the whole building."

At this point I tell my father I have to be off. Perhaps he doesn't even hear me, taken up as he is with his crutches. I slip quietly out of the door.

CHAPTER NINE

The Parody

In the kitchen I find Fausta standing over the cooker watching the coffee-pot boil. Without turning, and unusually for her, she asks: "So, did you sleep okay last night?"

I answer briefly: "Yes, thanks."

"Well I didn't, oh no."

I sense that I'm supposed to ask why she didn't sleep well. "Why was that?"

"There were noises coming from the study."

So, for some reason or other, Fausta is anticipating me, offering to satisfy my desire to know. I object: "Of course there were, my father must have been watching TV."

She says quickly: "He watches television with me. I turn it off for him before going to bed."

"So?"

"So, we'd already watched television, the eight o'clock news, then he ate his supper and said I could go. The noises weren't television noises."

So, this is it. I remember my father's remark about

women climbing on his bed with their dresses hiked up and realize that this is what Fausta wants to tell me: she wants to tell me that one of these women is Silvia. But I haven't time, and most of all I haven't the time it would take to turn a fairly loathsome piece of gossip into a calm process of finding out the truth. I say hurriedly: "Fausta, I've got to take my father his breakfast now, I haven't time to talk. I'll take him his breakfast, then I'll come back here and you can tell me all the nasty things you're dying to tell me."

"I haven't got anything to tell you. Don't bother with the breakfast. I'll take it to him this morning."

"My father's used to me taking him his breakfast. Come on, give me that tray."

She sends me a sidelong and clearly ironic look: "You know what you make me think of? Of the ostrich that buries its head in the sand and doesn't want to see anything."

She's right this time, and I say nothing for a moment, thinking it over. I tell myself that all my craving to know, to know everything, has, at the first hurdle, shown itself to be that quality that goes under the name of forward flight, fear of knowing masked under a proclaimed determination to leave no stone unturned. The fact is that Fausta is the only person who can tell me the truth about Silvia, and I am trying to delay this truth, even if only for a few minutes, with the excuse of my father's breakfast. Because I'm quite sure that what Fausta is about to tell me will generate the same feeling of horrified amazement I would have felt as a child had I seen the miracle in reverse of a snake coming out of the mouth of my sorrowful Byzantine madonna during the contemplative masses of my youth. Stupidly I object: "Ostrich? What do you mean, ostrich? Didn't you just say you had nothing to tell me?"

"I said that because deep down I feel sorry for you. There are some things a person doesn't even want to know, never mind say."

"But what things?"

"Enough, forget I ever mentioned it. After all, I'm leaving at the end of the month, so what is or isn't going on in this house isn't really my business."

I don't know why, but once again I back away from the real subject of the conversation and say: "I'll be sorry when you're gone."

"Honestly?"

"Yes, honestly."

"Why? What do I mean to you?"

I wasn't expecting such a direct question. I pretend to think, then say evasively: "This place is sad: two men on their own, father and son, both professors at that – they're not enough for each other. You've brought us the cheerfulness of a female presence."

She laughs to herself and says without turning: "Who says there aren't female presences in this house? It's just a question of knowing what time of day we're talking about."

Thus Fausta brings me brutally back to the subject that I have so far instinctively been trying to avoid. I realize that this time I'll have to face up to it and decide to do so with equal brutality: "What you mean to say is that those noises that kept you awake last night were due to there being a female presence in my father's room, am I right? Come on, tell me straight, just for once."

"For heaven's sake, I don't have anything to tell you, straight or crooked."

So, she's playing the dumb old game which consists of telling a juicy piece of gossip while at the same time pretending that it has been forced out of you. I experience a near-unbearable feeling of pain: it's a game for her; but for me it's my whole life held in the balance between loving Silvia and not loving her. Nevertheless, I go on calmly: "Listen, Fausta, I know what you want to tell me, or rather, what you want me to make you tell me: that my father had a visit last night. And so? It'll have been one of his many women friends, what's strange about that?"

"Oh nothing. Nothing at all. If you're happy . . ."

"I know perfectly well that my father is still a – how shall we say – still a very youthful man. There's nothing he mightn't get up to with these women friends of his. But even that isn't particularly strange."

Fausta stops playing and hits back quickly, going straight to the point: "What is strange is who let that woman in. Not me, because I didn't hear the bell at all. She came in like a burglar, on tip-toe. Your father didn't let her in because he can't walk. So?"

I hadn't foreseen this detective story-type objection. I suddenly feel the blood draining from my face. I stutter: "What are you talking about?"

"I'm saying that the person who came last night had the key to the flat."

I take refuge in an explanation that I sense will carry no weight: "My father must have given it to her a few days ago."

"No way. There are only three sets of keys in this house: you've got one, your father's got one and I've got one. Everyone else rings the bell."

"Right, my father must have given his set to a friend."

"Not at all. Your father's set were on his desk yesterday. I saw them there with my own two eyes."

"So?"

"So, you know as well as I do. There's only one other person has the keys apart from your father, you and me."

Before speaking, I think with desperate coolness of what

I ought to say and decide that whatever she tells me I mustn't let Fausta get the tawdry and shameful complicity out of me which, in the end, her revelations are aimed at producing. Spelling it out in a firm voice, I say: "Of course I know. The fourth person with the keys to the flat is my wife; and you would like to have me believe that she was the woman who visited my father last night."

"I don't want to have you believe anything. I never even mentioned your wife."

Did Fausta see Silvia? Since she only spoke of noises that kept her awake, probably not. Resolutely, I start lying: "There's only one snag in all this, which is that yesterday evening my wife was with me. Mind you, there wouldn't have been any harm in her coming to visit her father-in-law. But she didn't – last night she was with me."

She says nothing, busying herself with the coffee-pot where the coffee is rising with a hurried, insistent spluttering. A fine coffee smell wafts through the kitchen. Fausta opens the cupboard doors. She takes out two cups. Without turning, she says: "But how late did you stay with your wife?"

I answer violently: "I can't see why I have to account for my private life to you."

"So don't say anything and let's have our coffee in peace and quiet. You do want a coffee? I prepared one for all three of us, you, me and your father."

I feel the best thing to do is lie all the way. With fake reasonableness, I say: "After all, she is my wife and I've got nothing to hide. Yes, we've made it up, I was with her all night."

"Oh, you've made it up?"

"Yes, we've decided to get back together. We made love and after making love we slept in the same bed. Satisfied?"

She turns, holding the cups. In a pitying voice, she says:

"Poor Dodo, too bad I know your wife's voice so well. That's why I couldn't get to sleep last night. I heard Silvia's voice and I felt sorry for you."

I object: "Voices are sometimes very similar. You thought it was her voice, but in fact it was somebody else's."

"No, there's no mistake. It really was her voice."

"The fact is that you'd like it to be her voice."

"Oh yes? Why's that?"

I recapitulate, calmly: "Listen carefully. The door was closed, wasn't it?"

"Yes."

"So you didn't see Silvia in the study?"

"No, I didn't."

"You just heard a voice and now you'd like to think it was Silvia's. What does all this go to show? That you, for reasons I neither know nor want to know, don't like my wife."

She immediately retorts: "I didn't just hear voices, I heard noises, too."

I can't help asking: "What noises?"

Oddly enough, the question gets her angry: "What kind of man are you? You can imagine, can't you? The noises two people make when they have sex: soft, soft moans from her; real wild-beast sounds from him."

She's quiet a moment, then goes on: "The doors are old in this place, they don't close very well, you can hear everything. It sounded just like they were both in my room."

I come back stubbornly: "Maybe so. But one thing is certain – I was with my wife until dawn."

"Where?"

I make a mistake, but only realize when it is too late to save the situation. A shade automatically, thinking of all the times Silvia has proposed that we make love at her aunt's place, I say: "In the flat where she's staying now."

The victorious expression on Fausta's face tells me the lie won't work. She comes towards me with the coffee-pot in her hand, saying: "But I saw your wife as well as hearing her. I heard her leaving and I looked out of the window. It was three o'clock exactly. I saw her with my own eyes. Strike me dead if I didn't see her. She went out of the door and left, keeping close to the walls because it was raining. She was wearing a black mac."

I'm hurting now and I know it. I bow my head over the table and say: "As far as I'm concerned, you wanted it to be her you saw, just like you wanted it to be her you heard. The truth is that you didn't hear her or see her. You heard and saw somebody else."

She puts a cup on the table and slowly pours in the coffee. Then begins: "My poor Dodo . . ."

"Don't call me poor and don't call me Dodo."

"What do you want me to call you? You probably think I'm telling you all this out of spite. But it's not true. I like you, I really do. That's why I told you about last night; otherwise what do I care? It's their business, your father's and Silvia's. It's got nothing to do with me."

She's standing behind me, by my shoulder, and I can't see her. I pretend to think, my head still bowed over the table. In fact I'm not thinking at all: I'm just seeing in my mind's eye what Fausta says she saw: the street in the rain and Silvia, wrapped in the black raincoat I know only too well, coming out of the main door and walking off keeping close to the walls. Then, suddenly, beyond this truth which oppresses me, I feel I have found another, as it were, truer truth. Yes, the woman who walked off down the street was Silvia, obviously; but she was so in such a vital, free way that I can't help but love her, not just despite her betrayal, but because of it even, because of a betrayal that goes to make her all the more vital and free in my eyes. At this point I finally have the impression of having achieved the goal that, deep down, I had always set myself: to love Silvia as she really is and not as I would like her to be. I raise my head and say to Fausta: "Don't worry. I don't think for one moment you told me out of spite. I know you like me."

Since Fausta is behind me, I can't see the effect these words have on her. But the silence that follows makes me suspicious. Then I feel her big, warm, fleshy hand frame my face in a slow caress, and her voice whispers in my ear: "But you, do you like me, just a little bit?"

One never knows oneself well enough. Perhaps the effort involved in preferring the real Silvia who betrays me to the false Silvia who I'd like to be faithful, has exhausted me. Perhaps hearing words of love at this, of all moments, exasperates me. Suddenly, and almost marvelling at myself, I feel myself swept by a violence that is somehow experimental. I jump to my feet, turn to Fausta, grab her by the shoulders, turn her round, still yielding and amazed, bend her violently down at a right-angle over the table, her rump over the edge, cheek squashed down on the marble under the pressure of my hand pressing on her neck. At the same time I try to pull down her trousers and, in a conscious imitation of my father, hiss in her ear: "Tell me you're my pig."

But Fausta isn't Silvia, nor is she my mother. Her head, though forced down hard on the marble table-top, shouts angrily: "Ow, you're hurting me, what's got into you?"

I press on with my imitation: "Say it, say you're my pig, say it or I'll break your neck." This time she frees herself quite easily with a violent wrench and straightens, angry: "Are you mad or what? You hurt me. You really hurt me. What on earth's got into you?"

Ambiguously, I reply: "Nothing, I just wanted to check something out."

"And that's a reason for banging my head on the table?"

"Right, exactly."

Perhaps Fausta is already regretting having refused me. Gently reproachful, she says: "But why did you want me to say I'm a pig? I'm not a pig. I'm someone who likes you, that's all."

I say nothing. I stand there, silent, looking at the floor. She goes on in a lecturing tone of voice: "That's not how you talk to a woman."

"And how does one talk to a woman?"

"You have to be sweet, nice. Say kind things in a kind voice. Look at your father, for example. He wanted something from me, something very intimate if you like. But he asked in such an affectionate way I almost felt it would be mean to refuse."

Finally I say: "I'm sorry."

Fausta has now gone back to her usual amiable self: "You really hurt me, you know that? The marble was cutting into my stomach, I could hardly breathe."

Contrite, I repeat: "I'm sorry."

"So," she goes on tenderly, "promise me you won't do it again, ever?"

"I'm sorry," I say for the third time and head for the door.

I'm already out of the kitchen when she cries: "But don't you want your coffee?"

CHAPTER TEN

The Two Fables

❧

Once out of the house, in the street, I feel angry on two counts: angry with myself and angry with my father. With myself for having gone for Fausta as a result of a sudden, deplorable imitative impulse springing from rivalry and ineptly disguised as a psychological experiment. With my father for being the main reason behind this impulse. I'm so furious I scarcely know what I'm doing, I even forget the pain caused by Silvia's now certain betrayal. Or rather, the pain is still there, but mixed up in a humiliating way with the awareness of having wanted to parody my father's particular way of making love.

With these thoughts, or rather furies, in mind, I hardly realize that I've got in the car and am driving through city traffic. Then I start to race along the roads by the river, going from one bridge to the next, until I reach the place where I usually take my afternoon walk.

I stop the car by the parapet, get out and turn mechanically to the dome away at the bottom of the avenue of acacia trees. Perhaps because of the emotional state I'm in, I feel the need to rediscover thoughts which, even if they are catastrophic, form part of my normal life; so the idea of the atomic mushroom rising behind the dome of St Peter's comes back to me again. I ask myself what would happen if the bomb really did drop and I, now, immediately after having tried to rape Fausta as a kind of joke (a situation emblematic of my usual contradictory way of life), were to find myself witnessing the end of the world? But where would the bomb fall? Probably not too far away from the Gianicolo. The explosion would raze Porta San Pancrazio to the ground, likewise the statue of Garibaldi, the busts of all the famous men, the whole area around the Via Aurelia Antica, the Villa del Vascello, the Russian Embassy, the American Academy, Sant'Onofrio and the hundreds of buildings that climb up the hill. As for St Peter's, perhaps only part of the dome would cave in, so that the whole thing would look like a gigantic observatory. Inside the basilica, amidst the ancient columns now strewn about the paving, the statue of St Peter would rise from a heap of rubble with its famous foot worn away by the kisses of the faithful across the centuries. Thinking these terrible, mad things calms me down. Suddenly a cheerful, familiar voice makes me start: "What are you doing here? What are you looking at? There's no one around to look at."

I turn and see Pascasie, all hidden down to her feet in the usual red overcoat, watching me and laughing. Next to her, her deadpan eyes staring at me, Gesuina is holding an overflowing icecream cone and licking it thoughtfully. I answer abruptly:

"I was looking at the dome of St Peter's."

"Why?"

"Perhaps to take a photograph."

"Why take a photograph? There are plenty of postcards.

Who needs to take photographs of St Peter's? Anyway, you haven't even got your camera."

"I've got it in the car. You see, in the postcards they don't have that cloud that's climbing up the sky to the right of the dome."

"So?"

"So, I like that cloud. I was thinking of photographing it."

"You are strange, for lack of women you take photographs of clouds. Why don't you take a picture of us two instead, me and Gesuina, for a souvenir."

Souvenir of what? I hesitate, then go to the car without a word, get the Polaroid and turn to them.

"Gesuina, stand next to Pascasie, that's it, right up close. Pascasie, you put your arm round her shoulders."

I'm about to press the shutter when I realize that Gesuina has her tongue out licking her icecream. I say patiently.

"Gesuina, either the photo or the icecream, stop licking it."

Laughing, Pascasie exclaims: "Mother and daughter! If I had a daughter by John, I think she would be like Gesuina. When I was a girl I was all skin and bones like she is. I had long legs like she has and I liked icecreams like she does."

Not at all put off, Gesuina stops licking her cone and stares at me with intent eyes. I take the photograph, then say brusquely to Pascasie: "I was coming over to your place. Can I come in? Or is John there?"

Why this visit all of a sudden, when a minute ago I wasn't thinking of it at all? Why, no less suddenly, do I realize that I want Pascasie? Not so much out of revenge against my father, as when I went for Fausta a short while back, but so as to forget everything – Silvia, my father, Fausta and even the bomb. Oddly, I realize that what attracts me most with Pascasie isn't so much love-making, as the situation after love-making: her black body embracing mine in the dark; my body lost in hers in the shadows.

Pascasie immediately shows that she has understood; a calculating observant coldness appears in her dark eyes. Probably she thinks that in taking the photograph of herself and Gesuina I had Mallarmé's poem in mind again. In fact, with an obscure and almost comic allusion, so as not to be understood by Gesuina, she says: "Dodo, I'm quite happy for you to come. It's a pleasure. But I'm warning you, no poetry."

I reply with a gentleness that isn't affected, but pained, rather: "What unkind thoughts you have of me, Pascasie."

Curiously, the coldness in Pascasie's eyes is replaced by a kind of mild maternal affection: "Come on over. Instead of your poem, I'll tell you a fable."

"What fable?"

"A fable from my home country, a bush fable. Doesn't your wife ever tell you fables?"

Unexpectedly, my eyes fill with tears; the mention of Silvia has my emotions welling up in spite of myself. In a strangled voice, I say: "My wife will never tell me fables again."

"All the more reason for hearing mine."

I am furious at my own sentimentality. I realize I'm acting just like a typical adolescent who has been betrayed by the girl he loves and runs off to cry on mummy's shoulder. Right, because there is no doubt that just at the moment the abundant, matronly Pascasie is not the woman with whom you betray the woman who betrayed you, but the mother who enfolds you in her warm, protective embrace.

"Okay, let's go to your place and you can tell me the fable."

Then I pull out the photograph from the Polaroid and hand it to Gesuina, saying: "Here you are, keep it as a souvenir of Pascasie."

The girl takes the photograph, looks at it, then gives it to Pascasie and asks: "Can you take one of me, on my own?"

Jokingly, I ask: "Okay, I'll do you one, but won't you tell us who you're going to give it to?"

"I'll keep it for myself."

Pascasie interrupts: "Don't you believe it," she laughs, "she'll give it to her boyfriend. He's called Massimo. She'll give the photograph to him."

I say nothing and have the impression that the girl is embarrassed by Pascasie's revelation and grateful for my silence. This time though, Gesuina doesn't stop licking her icecream as I press the shutter. I pull out the photograph and hand it to her with the warning: "You'll come out with your tongue sticking out."

Pascasie says: "Gesuina, run off home now. I'm going to take a little walk with Mr Dodo."

Gesuina doesn't wait to be told twice. She makes a little curtsy in my direction, says goodbye to Pascasie and sets off, waving the Polaroid snap in the air. We watch her go by the barrier almost at a run. I turn to Pascasie.

"So, what about this fable of yours?"

"I'll tell you while we're walking."

She takes my arm, confidentially, and we go past the barrier and start to walk slowly along the deserted road by the river. Way in the distance, Gesuina is hurrying along ahead of us, still waving her photograph. Then, suddenly, she turns and disappears for good. Pascasie stops, puts a hand behind my neck and kisses me. I feel her mouth open up, moist and enveloping, like the sucker of some sea-creature; and I can't help but remember once again the simile in Mallarmé's poem, likewise marine, where the female sex is compared to a pale pink seashell. We kiss hurriedly and start walking again, slowly and silently, as if everything that is to follow had been settled with that kiss.

We reach the garden and go to Pascasie's door, almost hidden in the darkness at the end of an unlit hall. Pascasie shows me in, shuts the door carefully and puts on the chain. She leads me straight to the bedroom. I follow her and find her already by the window asking: "You want the light or the dark?"

"I want the dark."

The blind drops down hard on the sill. Pascasie pulls the cord for the curtain. Then it all happens in the pitch dark with hushed, indecipherable noises. All I know is that I'm getting undressed on one side of the bed, Pascasie on the other. No, I'm wrong. Suddenly I'm aware of her behind me, her naked, dark, warm body pressing against mine. I turn, push her on her back on the bed, plunge between her legs and almost immediately penetrate her, finding, unexpectedly, a vagina small and tight as a buttonhole. I stretch out on top of her, as if on a soft, warm mattress of flesh, and everything happens in silence, almost without movement, as though by imperceptible subsidences of my body into hers. Finally a low sigh, so soft I'm not really sure I heard it, tells me that Pascasie has had her orgasm. I have mine immediately afterwards in the same way, almost without realizing it, without pleasure, without movement. Then we lie in each other's arms, or rather, I stay there buried inside Pascasie with a feeling of abandon and repose, as if the night that surrounds me had taken the shape of her body for the occasion. Quite suddenly, I fall asleep.

I wake up, still in total darkness. I feel Pascasie's body beside me, but we are no longer embracing. We are side by side, not touching. In a loud voice, I ask: "Have I slept long?"

Pascasie answers: "More than three hours. I went to the other room, ironed my dress, watched TV, and you slept on and on; so seeing as you were still sleeping I came back to bed to wait beside you till you woke up."

"You could have woken me."

"You were sleeping so soundly."

We talk in the dark. Pascasie asks: "So, did you like my fable?"

"Yes," I say, "it was good."

"Perhaps it wasn't a new fable."

"Who cares: it's always new."

"When I was a girl, there was only one fable I really liked and I used to want my grandmother to tell it me at least once a day. Always the same one, I wasn't interested in any of the others."

"What fable was that?"

"It was a fable about a man who goes down into the world of the dead. He marries a dead woman, has a dead mother- and father-in-law, they have dead children; he works with other dead people in a shop for the dead and he gets rich doing business with the dead. But in the end he starts feeling homesick for the world of the living and he leaves his wife and family and goes back up to the living."

"Why did you like the fable so much?"

"I don't know. Perhaps because it gave me the impression that I could choose between two worlds: if I didn't get on in the world of the living, I could always take refuge in the world of the dead. And then the fact that there was another world ready to welcome me, if only I decided to go there, made me appreciate this world we live in more."

Slowly, everything comes back to me: who I am and what's happening in my life: Silvia, my father, Fausta, the atomic bomb. I feel Pascasie is right: there ought to be a second, reserve world, exactly the same as our own and always ready to welcome us when the one we're living in starts to go wrong.

I say with a sigh: "I've got a fable to tell too, but it's not a nice one like yours."

"You have a fable?"

"Unfortunately, yes."

"Why unfortunately?"

"Because it's a nasty fable."

"There aren't any nasty fables. In fact, the nastiest, the scariest ones, are sometimes the best, the ones you want to hear most often."

"My fable is really nasty and I wish I'd never been told it."

"How does it go?"

"It's the fable of a man who has a wife and she loves him and he loves her. But the father steals his wife off him, and so the man thinks he should kill his father."

"This is your fable?"

"Yes."

There's a long silence. Then Pascasie says: "The man must be you, the father is your father, and the wife, your wife. Am I right?"

"It's obvious, isn't it?"

She's quiet a while longer, then says: "I don't like your fable, Dodo."

"Why's that?"

The bedside lamp goes on. I see Pascasie looking at me out of the corner of an eye over her rounded, fat, black shoulder, her face a mixture of curiosity and what seems like amazement: "You want to kill your father?"

"I thought of killing him this morning, while he was sleeping. I was watching him sleeping, I didn't know then that he'd stolen my wife; but it seems I must have sensed it because suddenly I felt the impulse to kill him. Then and only then did I understand that he had stolen my wife."

Pascasie watches me, still curious: "You didn't know then that he'd stolen your wife, and yet you thought of killing him. What's that supposed to mean?"

I answer with a sigh: "Pascasie, we Europeans have discovered what we call the unconscious. Unconsciously, that is without realizing it, I wanted to kill my father."

"But if you didn't know then that he'd stolen your wife, why kill him?"

"It doesn't matter, Pascasie, you can't explain this kind of thing. I was looking at his cheek where he has a small wart . . ."

"What's a wart?"

"A mole, or something like that. So, I was looking at his cheek and then I felt a very strong desire to punch him or hit him."

"That still doesn't mean you wanted to kill him."

"He would have woken up and then, who knows? I would have gone for him, might have strangled him, even. But your father's body, Pascasie, is not like that of any other man. It seems sacred and if you think of striking it, you have a strange feeling, almost profane."

"What do you mean, profane?"

"Suppose someone urinates on a church altar; that's profane. But perhaps there was something else too: I had hit my father on the cheek before, when I was a boy."

"Why?"

"The motive was unconscious then too, that is I wouldn't have been able to explain it. Now I realize it was jealousy."

"You were jealous of your father?"

"Yes, I'd seen him making love with my mother. And, what's more, in the same way he does it with my wife."

"What way?"

"From behind."

"Oh, that's bad, Dodo. It hurts and it's bad."

"No, you don't understand, Pascasie. Not like homo-sexual sex. The way dogs and horses do it."

"That's okay, it's a way like any other."

Pascasie says nothing for a few moments. Then, still looking at me sidelong across her shoulder with her coal-black, cold, intrigued eyes, she asks me: "But why were you jealous over your mother? A mother is a mother, a son can't be jealous over his mother."

"You're right," I tell her, "but I was jealous and there was nothing I could do about it. This morning though, immediately after I'd found out he'd stolen my wife, I thought that my father wasn't my father, but just a normal rival in love. And then I didn't feel anything against him. We were two men fighting over the same woman and he had proved the stronger and that was that. But a father who is a father and who behaves badly – I mean in a way unworthy of a father – one can reasonably think of killing him."

With surprising animation Pascasie objects: "Oh no you can't! If you really can't help it, it's right to kill a rival, but not your father."

I start to laugh bitterly: "Why on earth not? Because he brought me into the world? A nice present that was! Or because he has white hair?"

Pascasie shakes her head with profound conviction: "No, simply because he's your father. There's a proverb where I come from and you know what it says? The son doesn't possess the truth, only the father possesses it."

"What's that supposed to mean?"

"That a father is always right."

"Even when he's wrong?"

"Especially when he's wrong. When he's wrong it's as if

he were right twice over: once because he's your father, and once because you're his son."

I laugh again: "This is the morality of the bush. I don't live in the bush. I live in Rome, in Italy."

Pascasie looks dreamily in front of her, as if in her mind's eye she were seeing the African village with the huts around the clearing and the great trees shading them. Finally, she says slowly: "I don't know anything about Italy, all I know is that where I come from, sons have to respect their fathers whatever they do. And that's because fathers know more than their children and if they do something they have their good reasons for doing it."

I suddenly remember my arguments with my father about the atomic bomb. I'd like to explain to Pascasie that the conflict with my father isn't just a result of his affair with Silvia, but also of our different visions of the world. But I don't know how to say it. All the same, I have a go: "Let's suppose there's a father who's a Muslim with a son who's a Christian; don't you think the son might hate his father for having a different religion from his own?"

She laughs: "You know, Dodo, back home we have Catholics, Muslims, Protestants and lots of others. But when things aren't going well, all these religions are too complicated and people go to the witch-doctor. He performs a little ceremony and everything gets back to normal. We're tolerant over religion. But a son has to respect his father if he wants his own children to respect him in the future. That's the rule."

I say angrily: "Perhaps where you come from fathers do know more than their children. But here, at least these days, children definitely know more than their fathers. For example, as far as the most important questions of life and death are concerned, I know more than my father."

"Life and death?" Pascasie asks incredulously. "Whose life and death?"

"Yours, mine, the life and death of people here in Italy, in your village in Zaire. Don't you know what the atomic bomb is, Pascasie?"

She answers seriously, looking at me out of the corner of an eye: "Of course I know. John often talks about it. We've decided that if there's a war, we'll kill ourselves together."

I experience a sense of surprise. So, I can't help thinking, I'm not the only one who sees the atomic mushroom sprouting from behind the dome of St Peter's; Pascasie has thought about it too, to the extent of planning her suicide in advance. Finally I say: "In any case, there's this difference between me and my father: he knows more than me about the bomb, but he had nothing against it being dropped. I know less about it than him, nothing in fact, but I don't want it to be dropped. That seems reason enough to hate him, I think. Add to that the fact that he stole my wife and you can understand my wanting to kill him."

Pascasie says nothing for a while, then says in a conclusive kind of way: "I can understand, yes. But the fact is, you didn't kill him. That's the important thing. In the end, you see, you're a good son and you've forgiven him."

I protest bitterly: "No, if anything, a good Christian. Or perhaps the most exact explanation is that I'm a good intellectual who isn't able to act: who thinks things, but doesn't do them."

Pascasie starts laughing: "But Dodo, why not accept the simplest explanation? That you forgive your father and your wife because you've taken revenge for their betrayal with me? That way your pride is satisfied. Dodo, I can read your mind like a book."

After a moment she adds: "But get dressed now, I've got a couple of friends coming soon to watch TV."

She's silent for a few seconds, then finishes with sudden

coldness: "I don't think we'll be seeing each other again for a long time. John's coming back tomorrow and he'll be staying in Rome until September."

CHAPTER ELEVEN

The Flat

❦

I've imagined Silvia sneaking furtively into my father's place after midnight; I've imagined Silvia explaining to my father her decision not to go on seeing him; I've imagined Silvia, despite this decision, once again letting herself be persuaded to make love; I've imagined all this and many other things as well. But when, a week after the discovery of her relationship with my father, Silvia appears at the bottom of the street and comes towards me through the rain, wrapped in the same black raincoat Fausta said she saw, all these images, so real a moment before, dissolve like overnight mist in the first ray of sunshine (the simile isn't new, but I can think of no better way of describing the effect that just seeing Silvia has on me) and once again I find myself entertaining some, as it were, optimistic doubts. Is it really true that the woman whose voice Fausta heard, and who she saw from her window walking off down the street, was her? And in any case, is it really true that Silvia and my father made love that night? Maybe instead – it's still possible to see it this way – she went to see him to tell him her "crush" was over and he accepted the fact? Though perhaps making love a last time before breaking up for good?

These doubts are not entirely otiose, not without their importance for me that is. I'm standing here in front of the main door to the block, waiting for Silvia so that we can go and visit the flat left to me by my mother. The flat is mine again now, but I'm only too well aware that in my eyes, and perhaps in my father's and Silvia's too, it symbolizes my renunciation of the ideology of my youth, my defeat. And if Silvia really has been and still is my father's lover, renunciation and defeat take on a particularly humiliating significance. If, on the other hand, my suspicions are unfounded, then the meaning changes ...

But here's Silvia. Her generous breasts seem to swell out larger than usual under the black, shiny material of her mac; perhaps she's pulled the belt too tight at the waist. After kissing her on two cold, rain-wet cheeks, I say: "I watched you as you were coming towards me."

"And what did you see?"

"That you have terrific breasts."

"Really? I think I've got breasts like a wet-nurse. You know what, though?"

"What?"

"It does feel odd coming back to your place."

I'm about to say: "Cut it out, Silvia, you were here a week ago and maybe you've been again since." But I hold off and restrict myself to asking gently: "Why don't you say, *our* place?"

Going ahead of me into the hall, she answers: "Because I'm still not sure what I'm going to do. In any case, I have to see the flat."

In his old wooden booth, the doorman, a yellowish,

shrivelled man in a dark-green suit that's too big for him, is reading a newspaper spread out on the table next to a very new-looking peaked cap. I knock on the glass, he raises his eyes to us, and I can't help wondering if he knows that Silvia sometimes comes to pay surreptitious visits to my father. I watch him as he looks at me from totally indifferent eyes and then makes a gesture as if to ask what we want.

I lean in and say: "You should have the keys to the flat on the third floor."

He understands immediately, opens the drawer, hands me a bunch of keys, and in a voice at once puzzled and trusting says: "Professor, you know the block, go right up. Or would you like me to go first and open the shutters for you?"

"No need. I'll open them myself and close them afterwards."

We climb a few steps and get into the lift. I close the doors, press the button for the third floor and lean back on the side opposite Silvia. The old, ramshackle lift starts to climb slowly, lurching and rattling. Silvia sighs. I ask: "What's up?"

"Nothing. I feel a bit upset."

Confronted with these signs of emotion which seem to be sincere, my optimistic doubts, as I call them, return once again. Is Silvia upset because the building reminds her of her nocturnal visits to my father? Or is she upset because it's the first time she's been back since leaving me? "Why are you upset?" I ask.

She answers with an ambiguous cliché: *"C'est la vie."*

The lift stops. I open the doors and we get out. Then I turn and say: "Yesterday, on the phone, you promised me that everything really was over between you and this man. So why are you upset? Unless it's not true at all and the affair is still going on."

Bowing her head, she says quickly in a tone which is almost of regret: "No, no, it's over, it really is over."

I insist: "I suggested you come and see the flat because of what you told me, or rather claimed – that this so-called 'crush' is a thing of the past. But if that's not true, then . . ."

I've got the keys to the flat in my hand, as though my using them or not were dependent on her answer. Still with that odd tone of regret, she says: "No, it's quite true. But it's still sad when something, anything, ends, don't you think?"

I don't reply. I open the door in silence. As soon as we're inside, I realize that due to the rain, the flat is looking at its worst. The hall, which is relatively small but with a high ceiling (it was larger but the lawyer split it into two different-size sections with a partition wall), looks ghostly in the dim light that filters through from the half-closed door of the sitting room. Torn strips of wallpaper hang from the walls; the floor is dusty and scattered everywhere with that straw they use to pack things into chests. "Unfortunately" – I'm almost apologizing – "it's not a good day for it today, but normally the flat's very bright, I can promise you that."

We go into the sitting room; the shutters of one of the two big windows are open, which explains the light that was seeping through. The wooden floor is covered in a layer of greasy dust, spotted with dark stains and strewn here and there with debris. On the walls you can still see the lighter areas where the pictures that decorated the lawyer's office used to hang. I say to Silvia: "It's got that squalid moving-out atmosphere, but you mustn't bother about that; you should try and see the place as it will be after it's been done up."

Silvia comes back quickly: "Oh, I can see very well how it could be!"

"And how's that?"

"It could be one of those old, aristocratic Rome flats. A big, beautiful flat."

So she likes it! I press on: "Yes, sure, once it's been done up this sitting room will be very comfortable. We could put in a fireplace, one of those big ones, sandstone or travertine."

"Let's look at the view."

She goes to the window, opens it and leans out with her elbows on the sill. I'm behind her, and I notice how, in this position, the small of her back dips down and her buttocks lift and stick out. Immediately I think of my father and the violent, compulsive temptation he'd feel if he was in my place. He wouldn't hesitate, I tell myself, to lift the black curtain of her mac up over the spectacle of her white buttocks; and Silvia, with the hypocrisy peculiar to this kind of sudden eroticism, would let him do it, without moving, pretending she was still looking down at the street. While my mind conjures up this image, as I lean out myself to look, perhaps I brush against her; or perhaps she's guessed what I'm thinking. Either way, she turns away from me abruptly and says: "Please, don't do that."

I protest angrily: "If he was here, you'd let him do it."

Without turning, she answers: "It's different with you."

"What's different? When you can't see a man's face, isn't he just like any other man whose face you can't see? If you had, I don't know, the doorman behind you instead of me, do you think it'd feel any different?"

This time she turns and I find to my surprise that she doesn't seem at all put out by my insistence. She says calmly: "That's precisely what I like about it: not knowing if it's you or the doorman."

Perhaps she realizes that I could feel hurt at this, because she adds: "What I meant was, you're right, men are only different when you can see their faces. Down there, they're all the same; there's no difference between the old and young, the handsome and the ugly. It's a strange sensation.''

"What sensation?"

"It's hard to explain. Maybe the feeling that you're not making love with a man who has a face, a past, love, but just with a cock, or rather with *the* cock, always the same, without a face or a past and," she finishes after a pause pregnant with cruel gratification, "without love either."

I've heard her use the term "cock" before, and always with a kind of gluttony, a greedy lingering on the two hard gutturals at the beginning and end of the word. I want to hear it again, as though to check my impression.

"Please, say it again: 'cock'."

Not especially surprised, as if she'd understood what lies behind my request, she says: "Cock? Why do you want me to say cock?"

Yes, just as I thought, she dwells greedily on the sound of the word because she's greedy for the thing it denotes. I answer: "Because you say it so well." I lean down and kiss her on the cheek. She pushes me away gently, and says: "But I want to be a madonna for you still, your madonna."

"Why?"

"I don't know, perhaps because that's how we began and I wouldn't like you to suddenly start imitating another person just because I'd told you about him."

I can't help thinking of Fausta and her reaction to the imitation Silvia is talking about. Then she goes on: "Now, let's go and see the rest of the flat. You know what, though?"

"What?"

"While I was looking down at the street, it occurred to

me that if your father had offered us this flat as a wedding present, a lot of things would never have happened."

"I wouldn't have accepted it then."

"Why not?"

"You know perfectly well why not: because I felt bound by the solemn commitments I made in 'sixty-eight not to own any property."

Heaven only knows why she likes to have me repeat these things; perhaps to reassure herself that, whatever happens, I'll always love her. And in fact she asks: "So why are you accepting it now?"

I reply with angry precision: "Because I love you. You wanted a house of your own and to get it for you I thought, fuck coherence, 'sixty-eight, the protest movement, dignity, my whole life, and I sent the lot of them to hell."

My sharp tone and crude language don't upset her. She seems satisfied. We go into the lounge. This room has an equally high ceiling, but is otherwise different, square, with just one window and a filthy, threadbare red carpet. Silvia stops in the middle of the room and says plaintively: "Oh, Dodo, you ruined everything, forcing me to live in your father's place. I tried every way I knew to make you realize I didn't want to go there, but you seemed deaf and blind and so you threw me into somebody else's arms."

A sudden suspicion comes to mind: "But when exactly did you, as you put it, throw yourself into this other person's arms?"

This time she tells the story straightforwardly: "The same morning we got married. You wanted to give me a surprise, remember? To show me our two rooms that you'd fitted out down to the last detail, secretly, without telling me anything. So, a half-hour before the wedding reception, in your father's flat, you said: 'Come with me, I want to show you how I've furnished our part.' I followed you, you led me down the corridor, you threw open a door and announced: 'This will be our bedroom.' Now I'd known for a while that we would be living in two rooms, but I hadn't seen them as yet. So, when you finally showed me them, furnished down to the last detail, my heart sank. I wanted to burst out crying. I'd dreamt of having my own house, and you offered me two rooms at the back of your father's flat. But I kept a grip on myself, I said it was a very nice bedroom, and I still had enough strength left to look over your study, the bathroom and even the broom cupboard. Then you said you wanted to go and buy some champagne to drink at the reception and you hurried off. A moment after you'd gone I left, still in my wedding dress, with my new ring on my finger and a bunch of lilies in my hand, and went to him. We made love, immediately, exactly the way you wanted to just a moment ago: me looking out of the window and him behind. While we were doing it, I dropped the bunch of lilies down in the street. I saw them land on the roof of a parked car."

I'm hurting and don't want to show it, even though I'm fairly certain she knows perfectly well she's hurting me.

"When I brushed against you a moment ago, it was by accident, I had no intention of making love. If anything, what comes out of your so detailed little tale, is a fact you've always denied till now: that the reason for your leaving really was the flat."

She admits it right away with cynical aplomb: "Yes, perhaps it was; but I really had got a big crush on the man. The flat problem gave me an excuse." She's quiet for a moment, then goes on: "Everything happened very fast, I left him and got back to our flat in good time: you weren't there yet. And then while I was waiting for you I realized I didn't hate you any more."

"Had you hated me terribly?"

"Yes, but only for a moment, the moment when you showed me how you'd furnished our two rooms."

"But why did you go on seeing him?"

She lowers her eyes and sighs: "I didn't want to, I swear, but every time I saw him I couldn't help myself, or rather, neither of us could help ourselves, because, as I said before, he didn't want the thing to go on either. Every time we'd swear it was the last time, and then we'd do it all over again."

So, it's true: my father really didn't want to go on with it any more than she did. This detail has a strange effect on me. For the first time I see my father in an unexpected light, as a naive adolescent who hasn't yet learnt to be ruthless.

"Look, I'm sorry. I can understand why you didn't want to go on with it; but why on earth should he feel he had to give you up?"

"Because he's fond of me and realizes that I love you and that my relationship with him can't go on."

I say bitterly: "You'll go on like this all your lives, swearing it's the last time and then going back and doing it again."

She protests vigorously: "No, I think it really is over now. We saw each other last night and agreed not to see each other any more."

I know she's telling the truth: it's the third time she's told me the "crush" is over (the first was on the phone yesterday, the second today). But I still have my doubts. I murmur: "Did you make love the last time you saw each other?"

She gives me an honest and surprising answer: "We did and we didn't."

"What the hell does that mean?"

"We half did it."

"That is?"

"But Dodo," she exclaims, "why do you always have to know everything? We half did it in the sense that he wanted me to kiss him there for the last time and to make him happy I did, but only for a moment. In the end, to be frank, I didn't do it so much for him as for his penis."

"His cock?"

"Yes, if you prefer to call it that. Because with him it's as if it were independent, separate from him, and beautiful. I kissed it goodbye, if you like."

"His cock?"

"Yes, his cock."

Now I understand the sad, lost, lifeless look my father had about him the morning after that other night-time visit. The physiotherapist had come in triumphant, waving the crutches and shouting: "A new life, Professor, a new life." But he didn't seem to share the man's enthusiasm. Doubtless he was thinking of the imminent and inevitable break with Silvia. I say brusquely: "Well, let's finish looking round the flat. This room could be our bedroom, especially seeing as there's –"

But she lays a hand on my arm and stops me: "No, I'd rather we didn't go on with this pointless visit."

"Why pointless?"

"Because even if your father's given you back the flat, it's still his, not yours."

I am irritated now by the idea that Silvia is falling into this easy symbolism: acceptance of flat equals continuation of her relationship with my father; refuse flat, end of relationship. Frankly, it seems a cheap correlation to me, not up to her standard. I answer coldly: "This flat isn't my father's, it's mine."

"It's yours, but at the same time it isn't yours."

"What do you mean?"

"I mean that we don't have enough money to live here without your father's help. And he's already helped you by giving you back the flat."

With a sudden flash of anger, I say: "You think more about my father than you do about me."

She looks at me with her primitive madonna face, pitying and sorrowful: "No, Dodo, I think more about you than about your father. But he's rich. With a flat like this we'll have to ask him for help in the end. And we'll be back where we started again."

"Back where?" I ask violently.

And I'm almost expecting her to answer: "Back with the love between me and him." Instead she says ambiguously: "We'd be depending on him again. He doesn't want to live alone. In exchange for the flat he'd ask us to eat with him, for example, or . . ."

"Or what?"

"I don't know. I just think it's unlikely that a lonely old man like your father would give away anything without asking for something in return."

"But let's think it over. The flat is big, yes, but we're not obliged to use all the rooms. We don't have to throw parties, for heaven's sake. It's quite possible to live modestly in a big, smart flat."

She looks at me with compassion, like an expert listening to an incompetent. "No," she says with conviction, "it's not possible. Partly because there's a kind of rivalry between you and your father, at least there is on his side, and he would never allow us to scrape and save, if for no other reason than to show you that he's the stronger of the two, precisely because he's the richer."

"You make out my father to be a great deal more generous than he really is!"

"Where there's pride at stake, even a miser is generous. And then there's another reason why we shouldn't take the flat."

"What's that?"

"A reason that's got more to do with you than me. You've always wanted to be different from your father, the opposite, even. He's perfectly aware of that. For him, the fact that you agree to live in a flat like this is a kind of victory. You stop being a rebel and become bourgeois like he is."

"What the fuck do you care about my rebellion?"

Her reaction is to mimic my own brutality: "I don't care a fuck about it. It was you who just said you'd sent all your life and principles to hell out of love for me."

I can't help being struck by the way Silvia uses foul language: it's as if the words were placed between inverted commas and kept at a distance by a gracious detachment. I say repentantly: "Forgive me. In the end I just wanted to tell you a very simple truth. That when all's said and done, between my politics and my love for you, love has turned out to be the stronger."

Without saying anything about my change of heart, she goes on: "In any case, if you want us to come and live here, okay, we'll do it. But afterwards, don't tell me I didn't warn you about the problems."

"So what do you want to do then?"

Her answer baffles me: "For the moment we can go back to living in your father's two rooms, on a temporary basis."

"What?" I exclaim. "A moment ago you said it wasn't good for us to be dependent on him."

She answers subtly: "It isn't good for us to depend on him as sham well-to-do people living in a flat like this. But as genuinely not-so-well-off people with nowhere to live we can accept his hospitality – on a temporary basis of course."

"So what's happened to that place of your own you ran off and left me for?"

"I realize it might seem to you that I'm being contradictory. I went away because I had another man. Now it's different: he's out of it now, so there's no reason why I should stay at my aunt's."

So, she's proposing that we go back to my father's flat where the opportunities for "doing it again" will be inevitable and frequent. What lies behind this proposal? A desire to go on with the affair? Or the strange but not illogical wish to put both herself and him to the test? Or again . . . Silvia is certainly aware of my perplexity because she adds: "I'm not asking you to decide now, right away. I went away to think. Now it's your turn. Go ahead and think, there's no hurry."

Then she finishes: "And now give me a kiss."

We kiss each other quickly, standing in the middle of the room that will not be our bedroom. Then we separate and Silvia says: "But now we ought to go and see your father to thank him and tell him we won't be taking the flat."

"Okay, let's go."

She takes my hand and I follow her.

THE END